THE GHOST IN OUR LOCKERS

By: David J. Brown

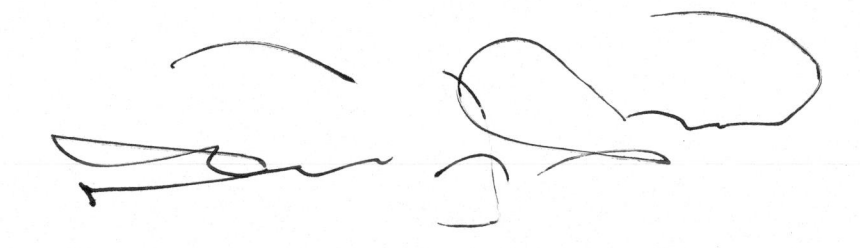

DAVID J BROWN

Published by: David J. Brown Books LLC

THE GHOST IN OUR LOCKERS

Copyright © May 2023

WEBSITE:
WWW.davidjbrownbooks.com

Proudly printed in:
The United States of America

God Bless America

DAVID J BROWN

This book may not be reproduced, transmitted or be stored in whole or in part by any means, including graphic, electronic or mechanical without the express written consent of the publisher except in the case of brief quotations in body and critical articles and reviews.

This is David J. Brown's 9th book and the 8th in his series of novels. Each book is a stand-alone novel but runs in a loose series with many of the primary characters moving throughout each book.

As in all of my other books, I am donating this book to be voice recorded and published in Braille to the United States National Library Service for the Blind and Physically Handicapped free of charge.

As in all things in life:

Never let anyone tell you that you can't do it.
Never tell yourself that you can't do it.

Dreams are worth dreaming.
Dare to dream my friends
and dream big!

Celebrate your blessings and speak of them often.

DAVID J BROWN

Be true to yourself and take chances. There are many days when faith is all you may have left, please know that faith for that day is all that you will need.

Within all fiction, lies a bit of truth.
Within all truths, lies a bit of fiction.
Our perceptions are the deciding factors.
David J. Brown

This story is a work of fiction. It is inspired in part, by true life events. In certain cases, locations, incidents, characters and timelines have been changed for dramatic purposes. Certain characters may be composites or entirely fictitious.

Introduction

Is death invited, perhaps even embraced by those who receive a death sentence via a physician, with supporting x-rays and lab results? How many people ask, (once they are given the diagnosis of a terminal illness) "How much longer do I have?"

That's a valid question asked by most all. Is that the very first sign of surrender due to our fears? Do we allow our illness to take us when it's not yet our time or do we take it on, head-first? Do we rush to the end for fear of what's between now and then?

Are we being self-absorbed or gallant in allowing ourselves to slip away quickly to help our families and friends adjust, so they too, don't have to sit day after day and watch their loved one's become nothing more than a sack of high maintenance and low value flesh?

How often have we read in obituaries that someone suddenly passed away unexpectedly? How many suicides took place because of the patient's fears of future sufferings? I don't have any of those answers but I asked those questions because it's no longer just about someone else. Now, It's quite personal because you see, now it's about me!

I knew there was something seriously wrong with me almost two years ago. I was thinking that I didn't need a professional diagnosis due to my family's health history, as I am the longest surviving male in my entire family's history. It stands to reason that it's my turn and I've dodged that bullet for twenty-five years longer than the oldest survivor in my family, on the male side. Hell, I consider myself to be a winner!

My symptoms are a culmination of several of my family members' blood diseases but mine is as much within my mind as within my body. I have always been physically and mentally agile and fiercely independent. Suddenly, two years ago, I noticed a slight stagger in my step, like I didn't have control of how I put my foot down and how I moved one foot in front of the other. I knew there was something out of balance and of course like most any other macho man in the world, I figured that I could handle this. Would things be different today if I went to see a doctor two years ago? The hard answer to that question is a firm no! It's just a matter of aging, if we're fortunate enough to live as long as I have with my family history, not to mention the careless way I chose to live. I pretty much would have called it all good in the last year. I've had difficulties with balance, with speaking with clarity and my thought processes.

THE GHOST IN OUR LOCKERS

What used to be my everyday normal is now a frustrating challenge.

Just this morning, I got caught once again, by Heather. Obviously, I doubled (maybe tripled) the coffee in the basket of the coffee maker. When she poured her first cup she paused as she saw the darkness in her cup, but didn't say anything. She took her first sip of coffee and acted as if everything was as it should be. As I poured my first cup, the smell alone told me I screwed up once again. It has been more than just a bit of a struggle in the last few weeks when I would set up the coffee the night before for the morning. We have a side site window for the water level and of course the basket for the coffee grounds. How many times, I don't even know how many times that I've had to make sure that I put coffee grounds in the basket. I had to make sure the site window for the water was up to full because I would forget that too. I would go to the refrigerator, take the coffee out, put it on the counter and just walk away without another thought. At some point later that evening I would go out into the kitchen and ask myself what the hell is this coffee still doing out on the counter, why didn't I put it back in the refrigerator? Then I would go and check the basket of the coffee maker, there was a 50/50 chance that I had not put the coffee in the basket. On more than one occasion Heather woke to a fresh coffee pot, full of steaming hot water. Either that or the coffee looked more like chili. She always did her very best to not make a face as she swallowed her, thick as chilly coffee. I had not only put the three scoops into the basket but at some point I added another three and who knows, perhaps another three after that. The coffee was of course not drinkable, Heather being the trooper she is, didn't let on so as to not embarrass me. With Heather's loving heart she would have sat through drinking that entire pot of coffee without saying a word so as not to upset me. Yep, that's another testimonial of what love truly is. I'm grateful to have her in my life, but at times, I wish she wasn't there. I wish she wasn't there to have to witness my demise.

    My latest book, "Betrayed My Body is Killing Me" was just published four days ago. I've made it very clear that this last book is in fact, my last book. I don't believe I have the mentality or skills to continue. I struggle to just put together the most common of sentences. I word search both in speech and in my mind for simple words. It's damn frustrating and in all honesty, it hurts my heart. I'm not ready to quit writing yet, but I know I have to be done. I know that I have to quit now before I embarrass myself and disappoint my readers.

    We've all watched professional athletes continue in their sport when in fact their skills are no longer what they once were. Their fans know that they're losing their edge but they still hold them in high regards for what they once were. I think it's sad, I think it's almost pathetic actually. Why people can't walk away at the top of their game, retire and live the life they deserve is beyond me. Whatever drives that I don't quite understand. Well, I've retired as an author,

THE GHOST IN OUR LOCKERS

not by choice but by situation. Others may argue that I'm quitting on myself. I have a number of readers that are pushing me to continue forward, they of course don't have a full understanding of my medical condition, some of them have no understanding at all of what's going on with my dementia, or even what it is. I have not made it public, only a few know but they're not ready to give up on me yet, they want me to keep going. Oftentimes I think they want me to keep going not for them but for myself. I have some wonderful loving friends. When I announced my retirement a few months back, I did not mention anything about my illness as it's not how I want to be known or remembered. I don't need or want anyone's sympathy. Some of my detractors may even want to say that I have now come forward with my dementia diagnoses to simply sell more books! They can think that shit all they want, I give no part of a fuck about them or what they think. Yeah, I'm a nice guy and I'm sensitive to people's needs and pains but I don't and won't let anyone kick me around. I have been a fighter most all of my life, now because of my diminished capacities I can no longer physically stand toe to toe with anyone, but I sure as fuck can still shoot them. There is a drive somewhere deep inside of me that tells me I need to keep going with my writing. I just have to suck it up, accept the fact that I need to spend more time dealing with my frustration and not become an asshole. My main concern today is about Heather's wellness. Yes, maybe I have to fake it a little bit and yes, she'll probably catch me, but I have to protect her and not amplify her current fears. So here I am back to writing, it's the only thing I know. What else am I going to do? I don't crochet and I don't hook rugs. I'll be damned if I will gather a bunch of t-shirts together and patch work a bunch of quilts. No, I'm no part of that kind of person. Card games and bingo at a senior center are of no interest to me, I'd rather eat worms. I must embrace my talents, God-given of course, not developed but God-given. These talents are my only salvation, hopefully it'll help me keep my mind fresh. Part of me says, "Save your mind, don't push yourself, relax." My fear is that I will fall into that Abyss of inactivity and I will unintentionally surrender. I can't allow that, I won't allow any of that, I will fight it to the bitter end, who knows I might even want to fight after that too!

    I have an old friend who's actually a classmate from back in high school that I reunited with at our 50th year class reunion. We've become good Facebook friends, she lives in another state but we email fairly often. She has read all of my books, when she heard of my retirement and again without mentioning my medical condition, just that I needed to do something else, she implored me to continue to write as it's helped so many others. Well, I finally leveled with her and she came back with, "Okay, you don't have to write a complete novel, why don't you just simply take notes like journaling to help others going into a situation such as you're in now. You're the epitome of what a true humanitarian is, you are a helper to so many that are personally affected by life's many ills. That is who you are, after all you have to know that you have changed so many lives by your giving encouragement to people that had lost their courage and their will to live. You are a true rarity!"

Then she brought the big question, "David why aren't you famous, why doesn't the entire world know about you? They should!" My only response was, "I don't have the resources to market myself and my work, so I rely on people like yourself and a rather large handful of others to carry my message through my writing and through my novels. Yes it's frustrating for me, I wish I could reach more people but I can only reach as far as Amazon will allow me. That and my website, which doesn't get a lot of visits. I mean after all, how many people want to know about the solution rather than whine about the problem? It takes a lot of courage to face your weakness and to make a determination to make the changes necessary to live free."

Chapter 1
The Delivery

I'm not at all surprised, hell how can I be? That's the way and the why of the way these people operate, it's always been their way and at some point, I allowed it to become my way too. It came as a phone call from an untraceable phone. It was a computer-generated message that said, "You will be receiving a package at your home by special courier in three minutes. Open the package and follow the instructions. You only have 5 minutes to respond to the instructions."

Then it was dead silence. My only thought was, "Ah fuck, here we go again, "The Company" is about to climb up my ass, take over my life, take over my home and use me like a rented mule, when they're done with me, they will all walk away."

If I would have had a stopwatch in my pocket and if I would have clicked it when I was told, 'within three minutes' I'm sure it was to the second that the sunglass wearing (overcast skies) dark suited wearing

DAVID J BROWN

delivery person pulled into my driveway in a rental car with a same looking driver and handed me the package. A slight nod of his head and without saying a word, turned and got in his vehicle and they drove away. Well, this must be part of the company's gig. That guy was far too together to be just a delivery driver, he almost marched as he walked. It was obvious that he has been a highly trained professional for some time.

I opened the package as instructed and what do I find? Another one of, "The Companies" untraceable cell phones, but this one did not have a keypad of any kind. There was a printed note that said, "Answer me in two minutes." There was not even a charger for the son of a bitch! So, I didn't know if it had a full charge or not.

I went out on the deck for a smoke, I wasn't half way into my cigarette when the faceless phone rang. I recognize the voice, the voice from a person that I've trusted and loved for more than six years now. Of course, that voice belonged to Amanda Robertson. Amanda, the lover that I've never had. In her most delicate of ways she said, "David, we all love you but we must be done with you. We all must be done with you. There is a dastardly plot afoot to publicly destroy you. We can't allow their attempts to wash over to us, please understand. They know they dare not kill you so they have to go after you and the only way they know how is, death by character assassination. David there are three attorney's that will be contacting you in the next hour. These are the

THE GHOST IN OUR LOCKERS

top of the top defense lawyers in the nation but I have to caution you, they still may not be enough. You see my love, you went too deep, no I wouldn't say that you went too deep by my or our standards, you went too deep by their standards. But then again these fuckers don't have any standards. That's right, I'm talking about the Democratic Machine. You know the machine that kills their own presidents, yeah that machine. Well my dearest, you've more than ruffled a few feathers, you've raised a lot of eyebrows and now they must destroy you, before you take them down. I can't go any further with this right now, the lawyers will explain it to you and spend a great deal of time with you. This, like everything else will not be easy, you at some point will receive a subpoena that you can't walk away from, you can't just take up your fishing pole and forget about the world.

They're driving the bus now and none of them have proper training or a license to drive that bus but they're going to drive it. David they're going to drive it right up to the end of the fucking cliff and you will be the only passenger on board. Don't let them kill you David, I love you, goodbye my friend."

It was one of the loudest clicks of a phone hanging up that I've ever heard because when Amanda said, "Goodbye my friend" I instantly knew that she said, "Goodbye for now and forever" and I believe it. I knew it at the moment with that all but deafening, click of hanging up with a cell phone meant the end. The end that was soon to break my heart. This was a much different twist this time, usually it comes in a phone call. Always abrupt, clipped and demanding.

I went too deep? I'm going to war with the entire fuckin Democratic (Demonic) Party? I'll be getting a subpoena? Three lawyers are going to contact me within the hour? For fucking what? I need a nap and about a dozen beers. I sure picked a shitty time to live sober!

So now I'm going to sit here and wait for the next hour for some lawyers to call, who of course I've never met nor do I trust. What are they going to do to keep me out of jail for nothing I've ever done? I don't like the way this smells, sounds or feels, there's something ugly going on, that's for damn sure!

Well the call came in less than that hour. It was a female voice, she said that she was calling to introduce herself and her associates who were contracted to represent me on behalf of a group of concerned citizens. Cute, who the fuck are the concerned citizens? What citizens are concerned about me that they're going to hire a group of attorney's for me and what are the costs? Oh this is going to be really interesting!

She asked me to be ready in the next fifteen minutes as a car would come to pick me up. I paused for a moment and said to her, "Just give me a minute of silence, would you please?" I set down my cell phone and walked into the kitchen, poured another cup of coffee, opened a fresh pack of smokes and went back to my cell phone and said, "Now young lady, I don't recall your name and as far as I'm concerned you don't need to have a name. You see sweetheart, I don't like lawyers, I don't trust lawyers, so what is it you are going to do for me?" She said, "When your driver arrives, you'll be taken to a meeting place where you will meet myself, my two associates and some of our support people." I said, "Hold on another minute, I want to digest this. I came back within approximately one minute as I said, "Here's the deal Hun, tell me where you want me to meet you, I'm not going to ride with a total stranger. This is winter, the roads are icy, the hills are steep and I don't know if you're going to pick me up to whack me or to feed me lunch, but I call the ball, as a matter of fact, if you're not okay with that, don't bother me anymore. I call the ball in every situation, no one's in charge of me, no one will dictate or force their will on me. You not only must be clear on that, you must be crystal clear! *Capiche?*

Now where would you like to meet? She suggested we meet at the Corker Hotel. I said, "No, not good enough, I'm too well known around that place. If there's someone that means to bring harm to me, they'll already know my patterns, nope not there. We will initially meet at a burger shop on the top of Piedmont Heights, so wherever you are now, I suggest you shag your asses to, "Big Daddy's Burgers." You can Google it, I'll be there in fifteen minutes, if you're not there in twenty minutes I'll leave, hence the, 'shag your ass.'

It seems as though I got the bonus plan. As I was seated and enjoying my coffee at, "Big Daddy's Burgers" in walked three very attractive, vested suit females who had 'snotty ass power lawyers' written all over their faces. Oh man, this is going to be a good time. They obviously had seen pictures of me because they walked right up to me. The place was pretty well filled up. They asked if they could have a seat and I said, "Sure, let's do that, have a seat ladies. Who's the coach of this team?" Lucky for me all three females were brunettes, one had bottled raven black/blue hair and hawk-like eyes. I pretty much figured that she was going to run the show, at least on their end. And sure enough, she gave me the nod that she was running the show. She smiled as she said, "Mr. Brown, could we just have a simple cup of coffee with limited conversation until we can decide where to hold our meeting?" All I could do was smile and say, "Yeah we can just sit here and I'll enjoy the view. Ladies, how did you get here, is it a rental car or is it one of those funky vans that changes colors?" They all looked at me strangely and I thought, well it sounds like they may not be a direct part of "The company" so this might be a little comforting. I said, "Okay ladies, quiet for a minute please, I need to make a phone call."

I called Tim and said, "Timmy me lad, you are available, right now!" Tim said, "The hell I am, I'm out in my garage working on a few projects, what do you need?" I said, "You have any of those extra vans laying around at the hotel in the garage. Tim said,

"Yes they're always there but I'm no longer working there, so I don't have any access to them." I watched the ladies as I said, I'll make a call. I need you to go down to the hotel and fire one up, fill the tank and pick me up at "Big Daddy's" on the top of Piedmont Avenue, we're going for a brief field trip. Tim giggled as he said, "You do know that I don't work for, "The Company" anymore, right?"

    Me: Fuck you Tim. Nobody gets to quit, "The Company." I know that and so do you, so knock off your bullshit, I want you to run interference for me. Dig around in your 'Magical Mystery Ship' and pull out your radio frequency scanners and portable fingerprint scanner, I have to guess that you still have access to some kind of facial recognition system. Bring your best laptop too, you are going to ID three vested suit beauties. I want to know when they cut their first tooth, all the way and up to what they had for dinner last night.

    Tim: Okay I'll be there in twenty minutes.

    Me: I'll be waiting for you out front, I will have three babes with me. Please bring, "The Noise" for two please.

    The ladies boss looked at me strangely and asked, "Are you going to let us in on what your plans are, and what do you mean by 'Bring the Noise'?

    Me: Ladies I operate on a need to know basis. I don't even know your names. How can you possibly need to know my plans? Clarity is my friend and it will be yours as well ladies, as soon as I know that I can trust you three. I call the ball in every aspect of every moment. I will control all movements and activities. If any of you have a problem with that, pick up your briefcases and take a hike. Who's going to pick up the tab for our coffee, I'm sure as shit not going to. Tip generously ladies, our waitress is a friend of mine.

Tim pulled up in an obvious Corker Hotel courtesy van. Stark white in color with tinted but not blacked-out windows, oh my, how refreshing!

Tim came around from the driver's side to open the side doors to let the ladies in. His sport coat was unbuttoned and I saw his shoulder holstered pistol, I'm sure the women did too. I smiled at the way Tim delivered his unspoken message. As he closed the doors after they got in I said, "We'll be with you in just a minute ladies."

I pulled Tim to the front of the van and turned my back, we stood shoulder to shoulder so none of them could read our lips, you never know about those slimy lawyers.

Me: Timmy, that better be a 45acp in your shoulder rig, if not you can borrow one of mine. I don't know who these women are, they supposedly have my best interests in mind, I am not quite ready to buy off on that yet. I will have them introduce themselves to you and give you their business cards. Run them through every resource available. We're heading up to the casino in Cloquet. I want you to watch for any tails, you know how to wheel a van, if you see anything at all out of character in traffic, just peel off and do what you need to do. Where is "The Noise"?

Tim: There is a UZI with a loaded twenty-five round magazine in condition one under both of our seats with a go-bag with six loaded thirty-two round mags.

Me: It's nice to see you back on the clock, buddy-boy!

Tim: Fuck you David, never again, I'm strictly doing this as a favor for a friend and nothing more.

Me: Oh really, then how the fuck did somebody just hand over the keys to the van parked in a secured garage? I never made the call to clear you. It was a test ole-son and you failed, don't feed me your bullshit. I'm sure that you probably had those UZI's just lying in your kitchen junk drawer, right?

Tim :   Dave come on now, just let me be Tim and you be Dave, okay? We'll leave all the rest out of it.

Me: Okay sport, when we get to the casino, pull into the parking ramp. While going up to the top level, change the color of the van with the hidden magic button and darken the windows. These ladies look like they could use some fresh air, we'll walk the stairs.

"Ladies, who's got the power credit card? Someone's going to register us for a room. This will be our meeting place until I change it, we could be here for a day, a week or a month. Who's ever carrying the power card go inside and get us a large business suite. Do not go back to the van, your pals and I will be strolling through the casino. Once you're registered, go to the room and call one of your compatriots here. Let us know what room you're in and we'll be right there."

The look on their faces was quite interesting, it was obvious to me that they haven't been in the game very long if they have even been in the game at all, then again they may be just that slick. If they are that heavily seasoned, I'm taking them to the poker tables!

I said to the two remaining vested suits, "What, you dolls don't like Cloak and Dagger sports? You people plot people's demise over cocktails and now you are going to play 'Follow the Leader'. Make no mistake about it ladies, I am the leader of this merry lil band and I am the only leader. You're going to have to lose those suits, you guys have nothing but neon signs over your heads announcing your power, hell your designer briefcases scream mega bitch all on their own. I don't want that shit, I might have Tim run you girls over to J.C. Penney's or Kohl's to buy some real people's clothing. Since you're all brunettes I think red's, pinks, blue's and yellow's would go nicely. Nothing fancy, everyday clothing, jeans or sweats are allowed but then again, some low top snug blouses and those painted on designer yoga pants would be just fine with me."

I got the look of deep disgust and it was not well veiled either. I thought, well if nothing else, this will be damn entertaining.

The call came in less than ten minutes that she was in the room. I called Tim to bring his bag of "I Spy" equipment to the room. The two lady's and I entered the room. I picked up the TV remote and turned up the volume as I put my pointer finger to my lips to signal for silence. I walked over to the windows and closed the blinds.

Tim was at the room door within five minutes of my calling him. He set his bag down and reached for his fingerprint scanner as he dropped the van keys into my open palm. I pulled out my wallet, took out my driver's license to show the ladies and nodded for them to do the same. Tim had his hand out to receive their driver's licenses. He scanned their finger and palm prints. I signaled for them to rise from the couch. They each reached for their purses as I shook my head. Tim put his hand out to gather the purses. As I nodded towards the door to signal the ladies to follow me, Tim was putting on a head-set with antennas on each side and pulled out a telescopic wand and plugged in a lead wire into each side of his headphones.

As I put my hand on the door knob to leave the room, I again put my pointer finger to my lips as I once again shook my head to signal for their silence. We rode down the elevator without a word spoken and I led them outside. I walked them to the van in the parking lot, opened the side doors and nodded for them to get in.

Me: Ladies, there is something more that needs to be done here, you need to lose those fucking hooker/power heels you're wearing. You all sound like a beer wagon team of Clydesdales in a street parade on the way to the National Western

Stock Show! Whatever you think your power is, you do not possess it here in my world. I have the power and no ladies, heels and designer handbags don't intimidate me. I don't give any part of a fuck what you paid for what, I'm not impressed. The way you three prance around, I can't tell if you're from Wall Street or Bourbon Street nor can most any others. I have to guess that by now you have come to realize that Tim is a bit more than just a van driver? That's right, he's my go-to guy and his credentials are impeccable, I trust him with my life, you three I don't trust to take out my trash and now we're going to get to that. That's right, Tim is running your ID's and he won't miss a lick, he's well respected within all the security agencies of the world, including Interpol and International law enforcement. If any of you have some deep hidden dirt you better spill it now. Expunged or sealed records are child's play for my man, Tim. I know who you say you are but I don't trust who you say you are and I've got a damn good idea of why you're here so let's have it. Are you here to protect me or are you here to take me out? Do you have those fancy little whore guns in your garter belts or waistbands? I know who sent you but I don't know if they know who you are, tell me who you are and I'll tell you if I want to spend any time with you, who's first?

    The lead lady said, "I'll take it from here ladies. David, the three of us are all well- seasoned Criminal Defense Attorneys in good standing with the bar. We are here to protect you but not as you may think. No, we don't carry guns, we don't need guns, we have other people who have guns the same as you. David there are people that want to bring great harm to you, they actually want to destroy you, they feel that they must destroy you. If they don't, they know that in time, you will destroy them. You have made a great number of enemies, you have called out some of the top politicians and other assorted crooks by name in your book, "The Judicial System is Guilty," and they know that if they can't shut you down and put you away, they know that they will be put away.

There is a dastardly plan afoot (still in the development stages) to destroy your credibility and charge you as a serial killer. They will do their very damdest to roll you up in concertina wire and bury you in the deepest and darkest prison cell and smear you with peanut butter and bacon grease to let the rat's feed.

      If they can make you look bad then the heat will come off of them. They want to kill you in the realm of public opinion. You have been very crafty (however not wise) to use the public and your readers to attack the enemies of the state. Understand David, that these people have their own rules and as you know, as you've even written about, the Constitution of The United States has been thrown out the window. Think back to President Trump's, "State of The Union Address" where Nancy Polosi stood and tore up her copy of the speech? You even said in one of your Facebook posts, "That bitch just destroyed federal property and should be jailed." As you well know, nobody follows anything to do with law or rules within the Democratic Party. Rules of law and the Constitution are merely words with no power. The power comes from the people but these people will not at any point entertain your right to exercise your civil rights, just theirs. We're here to help you stop them, we're not fighting just for you David, truth be told, we're using you to fight the good fight for all. You seem to possess a bit (allow me to emphasize the phrase) 'a bit' of decency. Mr. Brown you're a crass bastard for sure and we're not going to take much more of your bullshit, so we have to find common ground and in a hurry! Please understand that we're here to help you and the Republican Party along with the many disenfranchised Americans of both parties. That's right Sir, you are our 'rented mule' and we're going to ride you into the ground! What's in it for you? You get to re-establish your credibility, there's people coming after you that want to destroy every facet of your life and they're using your books to do it by using your own words! Yes, I know you have rights under our constitution and as you have stated in several of your books, that you have immunity as a writer but they won't respect that. Yes you're right, you do have that immunity, I believe you refer to it as having "Creative License." Well, that's fine but they won't respect that. So here's what's going to take place in a "Very large fuckin nutshell" as you like to say. In the next few days or weeks you will be arrested. Of course, it'll be under false charges but you'll be arrested as an enemy of the State, of course we will bond you out the moment they take you into custody. You will be taken for the longest, "Perp Walk" of all time. The media will be given full access to film you as well as receiving a media information packet as to all the charges in great detail. After processing there will be a lengthy hearing as to your many crimes against the state. More importantly, they're going to set the stage for all of the people's names and organizations in your books and claim that they became victims of yours and they will attempt to extract their pound of flesh. They will attempt to bankrupt you and keep you broke, if you were to live for another hundred years. Yes, it's all deflection bullshit but people listen to that and as you stated, (well stated as a matter of fact) that the Democrats are people who will believe whatever their party tells them because they don't have a belief system within themselves. They are weak, they're pathetically weak and operate on the only path they've ever followed. It's both family tradition and whatever the union dictates. You know yourself that it is a damn tall wall to climb over.

Chapter 2
Garters and Lace

Me: Okay ladies, who wants to take the lead? I'm here to listen to you. But understand that I take no direction from anyone, this is my show, my time and my place. If you dolls don't like it, you can hitch a ride back to the city with a taxi service. I don't want to hear any Sirs, I don't want to hear any Mr. Brown's, I don't want to hear any of that placating bullshit, my name is Dave, call me Dave. I don't care where you've come from, what office you represent, I don't need to know about any of your sheepskins you have hanging on your walls or of your corner glass offices. I don't want any of that bullshit. You've got business, I've got business, tell me what your business is, what are you here for and I don't care who sent you, I just want to know why you're here. Now what are your names?

The lead bottled brunette introduced herself as Doris, the tall one as Margaret and the other one as Phyllis.

Margaret: David you are known as a kind and gentle man but with glistening fangs. You are very protective of friends and family. You now must protect yourself as you would your wife Heather. This will be a fight to the death, your death!

Doris: David there are people that don't want you around any longer, they know they can't just take you out. You've exposed them already, what they have to do and what they're going to do or at least attempt to do, is to destroy your character. You will be facing several criminal felony charges, all fabricated yes, but they can make them stick because they're all part of the Democratic machine. They will hold open and televised hearings that will have to do with you being a suspected serial killer. I know, we all know it's a ridiculous stretch but that's where they're going. You see my friend, you didn't just ruffle feathers you plucked feathers and there are a number of people that if they can't discredit you they're going to go down in flames. They're going to prison and most everyone they associate with will be going along with them.

Me: Okay, now you've got my interest ladies, please understand that I don't trust lawyers. I never have and I've got plenty of cause not to. You don't strike me as do-gooders, none of the three of you do. So let me ask you first of all, who's paying you?

Of course I got the expected blank stares without a word. I said, "Fair enough, ladies, okay I get that. Now who are you going to save me from and better yet, who's going to pay me?" I got a bit of a chuckle from the lead lady Doris as she said, "You're being paid with your freedom. David this is not a game, these people want to put you down and they will use every dirty, filthy trick known to man and they might even devise a few new ones but this is not a game by any means. This is deadly serious and yes, they will go for the death penalty, now that we have your attention, go ahead girls."

Margaret: David we have to take a look at every situation that you've ever been in, where you may have upset someone. We have to start right from the very beginning of your life because these people that you upset may become witnesses against you and you can't defend yourself against them. You can't cross-examine them, they can say whatever the hell they want to say and it will go into the official record of which the prosecutors will use as a tee box on a golf course but what they're really going after is what you've written. They're feeding off of your writings. They have taken your novels book by book, chapter by chapter, page by page and gleaned anything that looked suspicious or that they could paint as suspicious. Let's start with your very first book, "Daddy Had to Say Goodbye."

Me: Oh ladies, just a moment, you do understand that I'm a novelist and you're all bright enough to understand what a novel is, even though it may be based on a true story? A novel is known as fiction. *Capiche?*

Do any of you really believe that they're going to try to prosecute me for writing fiction, where the fuck is my First and Second amendment rights and all the other amendments to follow? Anyone ever heard of creative freedom?

Margaret: David, you saw what took place as to what was called the December 6th Insurrection of the capital and they got away with it. Everything was staged, everything was programmed and well guided, they're going to do the same thing with you David. They're going to shit all over your freedoms, they don't care about your civil rights, maybe we need to go back and redefine what the Democratic Machine is. You're a bright boy, we all know that, but these people are all powerful because they're in power. There's no one to hold them accountable, It's no different than the federal government weaponizing all of the investigative branches and departments against the public. The foxes are guarding the hen house from the inside. Please, again understand this is not a game David. Don't fight us, we're not here to fight you, we're here to fight for you and if we lose you lose. We'll do our absolute damnedest not to allow that to happen. In summation, you could be expecting up to a 6-week trial. You will probably be arrested in the next 10 days and you'll be bonded out within the hour but they have to make a point of public record. We will be there for the arrest and all throughout the booking procedures. Don't say anything to anyone about anything. Don't comment about the weather, don't compliment anyone on how smartly they look in their uniforms. This is and must be a stoic time. This is about you having confused and glazed-over eyes, looking straight ahead and seeing nothing. Show no emotion or humor. David we've been briefed in part about who you are, your character and how you like to behave. You sound and look like a wonderful and charming man that we would all love to have in our circle of friends, perhaps in another venue but from today, up until the next year perhaps, we are all business. We have a number of associates that we're going to be bringing in from time to time to assist us but we are the three main people that will always be with you in any room, in any meeting. So you better get used to us and we have names by the way so I would appreciate it if you stop pointing fingers at us when you want us to speak.

    Me: Yeah, as long as I don't have to listen to a laundry list of your many pedigrees and all the wonderful schools you attended. What's your name again young lady, as I pointed to Phyllis.

    She smiled as she said, "Thank you for the young lady part, my name is Phyllis and I know you're going to jump right in and call me Phil and some other snide and snarky bar room bullshit, but you don't get to control me. Call me Phyllis please."

    Me: Phil it is, good copy babe, who's next?

    My name is Margaret.

    Me: Oh yeah I know a girl named Margaret, she goes by Marge and she is a total sweetheart. Margaret smiled and said, "You think we just got off the fucking turnip truck? David we've been on this case for the last three weeks, we've talked to most everyone you have written about. We have other people contacting your other friends. We've attempted to contact most every character in your books. We've talked to only a handful of them so far. Yes it was a daunting task. putting your character's names to real names but we made it. This isn't our first merry-go-round, it seems like you have a rather large fan base, but believe me when it comes to what you're up against you have no fans or friends."

    Me: Okay fair enough, Margie girl. So now we have a Doris, a Margie and a Phil. Now that I have your first names I still don't know who you work for, where you work, or where you live. I don't know anything about your family and I probably don't need to know, so you've read all my books, you've spoken to a number of people who you think you know as to be legit. How disappointed were you to find out that certain characters weren't real and in certain situations and several events never took place?

    Phil: David we don't have time for this, this is not play time and we sure as shit didn't come here to entertain you.

    This is deadly, deadly serious. David, in short and I'll be as lady like and as professional as I possibly can be, as I say this to you, "These slimy, rotten bastards are here to fuck your world! Let's start with your first novel, "Daddy Had to Say Goodbye."

Chapter 3
The Spooks

Thankfully, just as soon as I had had a complete gut-full of sitting and listening to that silly shit I got the text from Tim. He briefly said he had downloaded all the video tape with time stamps of our casino and hotel strolls. The women all look to be clear of any past criminal activity. However, they did fail to mention that they are deeply entrenched within the Republican Party and all are running for the governorship of three separate 'Blue States'. Minnesota is a stronghold with a stranglehold as a Blue State.

Tim: I'm done here, you can come up and help me carry this shit down now.
Me: Ladies, if we're done now, I think we can go back up to the room and you can gather up your things and you can head back to town. I'm going to go home and have a nap and yes you can have your own people drive you back. What, you think I didn't

notice your people shadowing us in the casino? You're talking to me about me doing a perp walk and I walked you in front of every pay cage bank of cameras in the entire casino. Casinos hold more cash than most banks, casino security cameras also have much better clarity than most banks! We've got more videos of you three than when you were playing soccer in your preteen years. Yeah, you all check out but I still don't trust any one of you. What that is going to take, I don't even know. I'll know when I know and then I'll let you know, but for now you are impinging upon my nap.

    Doris: Yes slick, we saw what you were doing and we still don't trust you either. I think it was a cool move for you to put us into a white van and then to put us back into a blue van but it was all the same van. That color change was really interesting. How do we know? We each tucked something under the seat of the van in case some dastardly event took place and we came up missing. Yep, it looks like trust is going to be a real problem here. I hope we can survive it. Go have your fucking nap, I will call our people for a ride, they're better drivers than Tim anyway!

    Me: Don't hand me that line of bullshit, they were nowhere to be seen as we were driving so obviously, they have a tracker on your cell phones. That's real cute but that's old school in this day and age. I suggest you ladies focus on defending me and not trying to figure me out. I'll tell you who I am when

DAVID J BROWN

I'm ready to. Text me your cell numbers and your messaging email addresses. I'll let you know about tomorrow, when and where, good day ladies.

Oh and one more small item ladies. I suggest you all add a double splash of truth serum with your morning coffee. Lastly my loves, I want two crisp stacks of $100 dollar bills banded in two bundles totaling $20,000. Tim does not work for free.

Chapter 4
The Dance

    I never got that nap that I went home for. I decided that I would play along, at least for a while, with these dolls. I didn't know how far I wanted to go or how much of their bullshit I actually was going to try to believe. Try, that is, try to believe.
    I had to think about these women, they seem to be a little slipperier than I'd like but I understand what their jobs are and no, they don't put all their cards on the table at any one time and neither do I. I get that but there is something different about one of them. While there's no question that Doris has the power. Doris and Marge I think are kind of like bookends. They support each other but yet they'll do combat within themselves but Phil seems to stand a bit apart. I think there's something quite different about Phil, she seems to come from a different mold as the other two.

As in every case in my life, I measure everyone I come into contact with. Whether I'm at the gas station, grocery store, clothing store or an AA meeting, sometimes even in traffic. I look at people as to the potential of them to bring harm. I want to know what people are about before they show me. We're back to being always alert as in, forewarned is forearmed. So what I noticed about Phil is that when I was speaking she couldn't look at me directly, she held her eyes down or even over my head but she couldn't look directly at me. Yet when other people were speaking to me she watched me intensely. I don't know if she's a studier for the team or for herself. I'm not quite sure of what her game is but she's paying close attention to me and trying not to get caught by me or maybe even by them as well. But there's something about her or something about Phil that bears watching. Is she friend or is she foe, is she trying to bring forward a message and what level of message is it? This will prove to be interesting for sure but Phil is the one I'll be watching for. Things now point to where I need to separate Phil from her two pals and have a one-on-one. I think she's holding a hole card, I Sure as hell hope it's an ace!

I had them meet me in the lobby at the Corker Hotel. They were already staying there. What the hell, I still have full access to the top level of my former "Eagles Nest" so what the hell. Tim didn't seem at all happy about my re-employing him until the next morning when I had the ladies put the two stacks of $100 bills totaling twenty grand on the table. I slid it over to Tim as I said, "Maybe you could buy your wife a nice dinner tonight, shut the fuck up, you're back on the clock!" I turned to the three legal beagles as I said, "Ladies, do you recall my final statement from our little gathering yesterday?"

Well ladies, this is your one opportunity, lie to me again and we're done. I don't give a fuck what your purpose is, I want the truth, so tell me this, how is it (and I'd like to see those business cards of yours) that state that you are working for a movie production company and you're getting background on me and my writing for a full-length movie? That's really fuckin cute, so you met with the number of my friends and gave them a bullshit story about making a movie about my life?

Tim looked over at me and showed just a bit of astonishment as to how I was able to dig up that information and he wasn't. I just smiled back and said, "It's all about connections pal, it's all about connections. Now ladies before you step into a massive bear trap I strongly suggest that you write up a contract between yourselves and myself. That was pretty slick the way you walked around passing out your business cards to my friends and acquaintances announcing that you're representing me when we haven't had any type of agreement or a signed contract. You may be in good standing with the bar only because you have not been caught yet. That's a wonderfully creative way that allows you to stand away from me and not have to honor a client-attorney privilege. So for right now, Timmy and I are going to sit here and count his money because I still don't trust any part of what any of you are about. You best be pounding out that contract now! I will have three friends stopping by in the next 20 minutes that I would like you darlings to meet. Yes, one is a Federal Court Judge the other is an active District Court Judge and the third is an attorney who has the biggest of all sticks in the entire state. They're just going to swing by to examine your contract with me. Oh and by the way, I dig the way you all have your hair in ponytails and you're wearing those spandex things that make you look like college cheerleaders.

My legal friends all came by at the same time, they each read the contract between the Attorney/Client. All three thought it should hold up in any court. I smiled and asked if they could add one thing, that one thing being and reading, "As if at any point, the client suspects any level of fuckery by the client attorneys, the listed attorneys will be charged in Criminal Court. My federal judge buddy said, "Yep that can go in there, that's perfectly legal and binding. If you ladies would like to sign it, we three are here to witness your signatures to the agreement with our friend Mr. Brown and let me add this ladies, you fuck with him, you fuck with us, and you will pay. He will see to it and so shall we."

There sat three bespeckled ponytail cheerleaders who had just been handed the spanking of a lifetime, you could almost hear their bones rattle as they shuddered. My guests left and it was time to get down to business.

Me: Ladies before we begin, I would like to make a statement and I'm hoping that you'll pay very close attention. I'll start with a quote by George Orwell which reads; "However much you deny the truth, the truth goes on existing." Okay and something else I've seen over the years and I don't know where exactly it came from other than the internet it talks about the, Lie:

"The Lie said to the Truth, "Let's take a bath together, the well water is very nice. The Truth, still suspicious, tested the water and found out that it really was nice so they got naked and bathed. Suddenly the Lie leapt out of the water and fled wearing the clothes of the Truth. The Truth climbed out of the well to get her clothes back, but the world upon seeing the Naked Truth looked away with anger and contempt. The poor Truth returned to the well and disappeared forever, hiding her shame. Since then the Lie runs around the world dressed as a Truth and society is very happy because the world has no desire to know, "The Naked Truth."

Toxic individuals look for drama, they live for drama. If they can't find it they create it and of course it has nothing to do with the truth. I have saved a lot of people's reputations by not telling my side of the story. It's my only chance for humility.

So ladies please understand that I have no time or room for anyone's bullshit, with knowing that, let's have it ladies who's first?

Phil: David, my God, you carry a power that is uncommon to any of us three. When you make friends, you really do make friends! Well let's get right to, "Daddy Had to Say Goodbye." I want to start with the reader's praise and reviews. I very much enjoyed your note from the author which reads, "My agent was appalled when I submitted the book reviews from legitimate readers and friends. According to your agent only people who have prominence, fame and stature should be used for book reviews. I very much enjoyed the gasp and rapid eye blinking when you said, "You are fired!"

That was a beautiful way to set the stage, you immediately identified your power and your passion. Your first review was by RW Clark which read in part, "It will cause the most casual of readers to examine their moral compass." That's another power statement. You published fourteen reader reviews in your first book. They were all grateful and sensitive to what you were offering them, so that's a huge win that we can use.

You go from there to thank your friend Lydia and as well as your website designer and artist, Angie Simonson for their work. Your three-line dedication to the women of your past was gut-wrenching. That statement read, "With thanks to the women that loved me, for as long as they could. To those people that love me today, no matter what." That again shows the sensitivity and humility of a strong but severely broken man. Just below that, in the same page you wrote, "Within all fiction lies a bit of truth. Within all truth lies a bit of fiction. Our perceptions are the deciding factors." Your brief twenty-three line introduction would bring most all readers to their knees and they would find a sorrow that they may have never known before. David there is absolutely no question in anyone's mind what a phenomenal writer you are, but knowing that it's your life story, I am amazed with what a phenomenal survivor you are. You took your pain and put it on the table for all the world to see for the sole purpose of hoping that they will recognize themselves and lay their own pains on the table and grow from it. David, your first several chapters lay out the makings of how a serial killer is made. Nobody can imagine that kind of pain and that kind of heartache, the loneliness, the darkness, the hunger, the sickness and the beatings and the fear of your next beating being even worse than the last one. You even write about wanting to kill people that were mean to Donnie, people that teased you about being an oppy and a retard. Jesus Christ David, you beat up a Catholic Nun! You didn't hit her just once or twice, you even wrote about how you had to be pulled off of her as you were throwing and landing haymakers left and right. Once the other Nun got you off of her, you still kicked her before they could pull you away. Yes, that sounds like the makings of a madman all right. The disappointment and the heartache of having to quit the Cub Scouts, that you worked so hard to earn the money to buy your merit badges, I could almost see you dropping your merit badges into the trash (with seeing your tears streaming down your cheeks) because your mother wouldn't tend to your simple needs of having your patches sewn on your shirt, your greatly faded, used Cub Scout shirt, at that! I was thinking that this was going to be a confession to killing your mother and your father. That thing about stealing your landlord's saw out of his shed and cutting down a man's Christmas tree in his front yard to help your mother feel better. That shows that you had a very sensitive heart even to your cruel abusers. The way the police department interacted with you and you're recognizing them for what they did shows the tender-hearted and grateful child. This is where things get so confusing, one part of you is so loving, sensitive and respectful. Then there's another part of you that is full of hate and rage. So David, I have to ask you because I know the attorneys are going to ask you and they're going to even suggest that maybe you suffer from dual personalities. Have you ever been diagnosed with dual personalities?

Me: No, I haven't. I have never been diagnosed with a goddamn thing other than I have dementia and that's just recent.

Marge: When it comes to your grandmother with the big dogs, I think that every reader that picks up your book wants to kill that filthy drunken redheaded bitch. I believe you referred to her as "Jiggles?" Your love and respect for your grandma's husband, Jim was quite apparent and that tells us that you do know how to bond with others. The same follows for the Watkins man and Mac the shoe and ice skate repairman. Your stealing money from the UNICEF boxes will raise a few eyebrows and I'm sure you'll be labeled as a thief in training. The Heartbreak of Mac closing the shop and having to watch two men drown while smelt fishing would have destroyed most any child, let alone the adults who witnessed that. Your statement that you wanted to go to the bar with your dad and have some beers so you could feel better too, pretty much lays out how you became an alcoholic, it's apparently a learned behavior. In your case, it's what you witnessed and knew that alcohol was the only thing that could make you feel good or at least not feel so bad. And David, this rolls right into your father taking you fishing with the rest of the family, you falling into the spillway and actually enjoying the effects of drowning, you welcomed that, David! That tells me that you suffered more than could ever be measured. To me, that speaks of a child and a man that needed to be understood and loved. It will tell the other team that you are suicidal maniac. You go on to tell how your mother wouldn't comfort you sitting on that frozen rock with your jeans frozen to your legs and she wouldn't even look at you, nobody would talk to you, they let you sit there and suffer. Yes, that would make me bitter, that would make me rageful and it might even make me homicidal.

   Me: Let's take a break, I'm going for a walk. I expect you all to be sitting here when I get back. Help yourself to anything in the kitchen. Restaurant menus are in the top drawer next to the dishwasher on the right. You can call down to room service anytime you want.

Chapter 5
Settling In

    I returned to the Eagles Nest a half hour later. The ladies were enjoying a bowl of popcorn. I said, "Ladies, let's just get this right, right now. Everything you've read in my first book is absolutely 100% true. The only thing that makes that book a novel is I've changed the location's and the names to protect others and myself from legal liabilities but the stories are all true. The first hundred pages of, "Daddy Had to Say Goodbye" in- fact, took place right here, in Duluth Minnesota where we are now. If you've not figured it out yet, I am the character Clinton Flanagan.

    I propose we do this, you just ask me whether or not the situations or names are real or false. That will save us an awful lot of time. Please keep in mind that I'm a former police officer, I've been to court many times. I've testified in court and have had people that I have arrested or even ticketed for traffic violations turn into absolute fucking lying monsters.

The sweetest looking little granny will go to court and claim that I tried to look into her blouse or that I tried to proposition her with my fly down. They'll do anything to get out of a ticket and then the next day they'll go to church and act holy as hell, so nothing's going to surprise me. You needn't warn me about what they're going to do, I've got a damn good idea of what they're going to do. Yeah and you wonder why I detest slime ball lawyers? It's always about the win, it's not about the facts or even the truth, it's about the win and they don't give a fuck who they harm, who they put away or who they bankrupt as long as they get paid. So we started with chapter #7 I believe, let's move on to that.

      Doris: David I concur with everything you just spoke of. We have an awful lot of territory to cover, the level of which these bastards will stoop to, is bottomless. We have little doubt that they will find victims from your past and your writings. There will undoubtedly be people who have suffered PTSD due to your writings. People that have never even seen or looked at your books, let alone read them, will suddenly become greatly harmed. They'll find themselves as victims of course and these victims will want to be reimbursed for their suffering. Let's remember that these bastards have the doors wide open to the biggest vault in the world. They have full access to unlimited funds of the U.S. Treasury, which means of course, unlimited funds equals unlimited power and corruption as you well know. Just so we're clear, this whole thing was brought forward when you

THE GHOST IN OUR LOCKERS

exposed the children's food program fraud in Minnesota along with your assertion that Minnesota Democrat Representative, Paul Wellstone and his family were murdered by his own party. I now understand that there are sixty people that have been arrested who were directly involved and knowingly received stolen money in this $250 million dollar children's food scam. I don't know how in the hell the Governor and the Attorney General can claim not to know anything about this massive fraud. When the public did find out, the governor claims the FBI told him to stay out of it. Well, that's the machine, that's how they work. Okay, on to chapter #7.

    Me: Margie girl, you've been awful quiet. I want to hear from you, what's your take on everything?

    Marge: David, I've never represented a client with a level of intelligence and gut honesty that you possess. At times you frighten me, your language is oftentimes appalling. I understand how your friend, "Granny" becomes disgusted with your verbiage but she still loves your writing. Yes I understand that whole thing about sentence enhancers. I think that's just an excuse for you to talk like a filthy bastard. Of course, I'm smiling as I say that. David, I love your writing, you're brilliant, absolutely brilliant. I think this trial will be your breakout debut as an author. You will need an agent to book all of your personal appearances and your book sales will go right through the roof or as you might like to say, "Right through the fuckin roof," we're all on your side. David, we want you to be a part of our team, we have to be a team, we can't have one against three, we've got to have four against the world. Please cooperate with us, let us do what we know how to do. Remember we've got a dog in this fight too, that's right, I hope to be the next Governor of the state of Minnesota and you my friend are going to be my meal ticket. After the truths come out and those of course are your truths of democratic politics, the people that are Die-Hard Democrats will leave the party with disgust, once everything is exposed. No they may not vote for me but they sure as hell won't vote for another Democrat. They'll probably just stay home or go fishing. I fully expect a landslide victory. So that's the dog in my fight, my other two associates are going for the governorships for both the state of Michigan and Wisconsin. We're going to not just start an avalanche, we're going to do a major cave-in on the whole damn Democratic Party. We can do that with you David, truth be told we have been searching for the last five years for someone like you to champion. Someone we could hold up to the public as a kind and loving individual, a man with deep morals and a strong commitment to protect the weak and the righteous. I saw where you wrote the other day on Facebook and made reference to a police officer killing a bad guy that shot at the officer and actually wounded him. You wrote, "When evil calls.... the righteous will answer." Well that's you, without question, that's you!

    I would like you to believe that that is also us. We don't need money, we don't need power but we need the power to win the governorship of each of our respective states. You, my friend, are our only hope.

Me: Oh is now the time for a group hug, any guitars in your pockets? Maybe we could all join hands and strum a few cords of Kumbaya as we rock back and forth sitting on the floor. Shut up with that shit, we've got work to do, let's do it!

Doris: David, can we take a brief break, we set up a workstation downstairs in the Seafarer Room that we would like you to look at. I smiled, reached for a handful of popcorn and said, "Yeah let's go ladies, show me what you got."

When we went to the Seafarer Room the first thing I noticed was that no one put a key into the door lock to open the door which pissed me off greatly. If they've got something to show me that relates to any part of this deal, it should have been secured and this room is not a secured room, even though it has locks and cameras. Cameras don't stop crime, they just record crime. What the fuck is going on with these broads? When I entered the Seafarer Room there were the same number of grease boards hung from the ceiling with a lot of different writings with another twelve boards on floor easels. Those floor easels actually wrapped more than half the way around the entire room. I asked, "What is this Doris?"

Doris: David we sat up half the night last night laying this all out, this is our strategy in part and I think this would be a good room to work through it.

Me: No dice ladies, absofucking-lutely not! If this is as serious a matter as you try to lead me to believe, this has to go into a highly secured area. This door wasn't even locked! Anybody could have walked into this room and we don't know that somebody didn't! So now we're going to have to ask security to view all the tapes, nice work girls, leave shit the fuck alone! I want these boards to come down immediately!

Doris: David I will have these removed immediately, I'll call maintenance right now.

Me: The fuck you will, you gals put this shit up here, you're going to take it down. You're not calling anybody for anything, you don't call the ball on anything in this building other than the way you want your bed covers turned down at night. You have no power or no say with any of the staff in this facility. I hold the power, you see girls, there's a thing called respect. I've earned the employees' respect of this facility, they call me their friend, I call them my friends. You can bring up any employee in this entire building and I will tell you how many children they have, their children's names, their ages, their pet's names and where they go to school. You see, when you embed yourself into another person's life, you do it because you care for them, not because you want to use them. *Capiche?*

Now you three dolls go get a few Guest luggage carts, you load all these easels and grease boards on the carts, cover them with bed sheets before you leave this room and you will wheel them to the elevators and you will take them up to the, "Eagles Nest." If I have to give any one of you, just one more lesson in the humility department (that you're all so greatly lacking) we will call it good, good as in fuckin done! This whole thing will be over, I don't give a fuck! If people want to come at me, let them come at me, I don't need a bunch of big mouth lawyers dancing around and if you think for one moment that my federal judge friend was bullshiting you, let me assure you of something. The only work you'll ever get again in your entire life, will be defending a client who has a Karen that runs their Homeowner's Association and you'll be going up against her for violations such as, too high of a lawn and a couple dandelions. That will be your life's career, don't fuck with me, don't fuck with my friends and don't try to bullshit me, so that's it girls, final warning!

One other thing ladies, it wasn't just the three of you that were in this room last night. There was a fourth and that fourth was a female. Let me explain something to you all. Men have a different set of senses than women, my greatest sense is my sense of smell. When that door opened a few minutes ago, I smelled a memory of an all but faded odor, of a woman's perfume. Not any of yours and yes I know who that woman is. You see girls, a thousand women could put on the identical perfume and each would have its own individual signature scent to a man that loves that woman. Yes, she was the love of my life many years ago, but sadly I had to walk away. Not that she wasn't the absolute perfect match for me, it was that I was far too broken for her innocence and naivety. What was so breathtaking was her beauty and her loving heart. But no, I was too dark for her. I could not risk harming her in any way. I don't know what you dolls were up to with her and I don't need to know, if I do need to know I'll go to the source but I want you to leave my friends the fuck alone, this is our battle to fight, not theirs.

    Marge:　But David, so many people adore you, we have three, four inch binders full of your readers reviews and personal letters that they sent to you and how you affected their life and how they are living in a emotionally and spiritually free world today because of your relationship with them and your writings. We desperately will need those people to testify on your behalf.

    Me:　No dice ladies, that's not how it's going to roll. If they want to take me down they can take me head on. They're not going to fuck with my people, that's right everyone, my people! Yes I have people too, but my people don't always have the power and the ways that your people might have. You see ladies, my people have love in their hearts which they extend to others, you three do it for a dollar, they do it for free.

    You three are not the same caliber as my people.

Chapter 6
Only Fools Trust

That same feeling kept coming over me, I couldn't shake it. I know better to ignore my senses but none of it made any sense, none of it! So what the fuck are these women up to? Is it possible that they are actually batting for the other team? Is this whole thing a set up to where when things get to trial they become witnesses and not attorneys? Yes I know they check out with a bar but this is for all the marbles, this is big people shit, this is power shit and Democrats have no compunction with who they harm or even who they kill. I think some of the Clinton's and Obama's history should bear that out.

What is their game? They told me early on that they were going to use me as a springboard to propel themselves into the governorships of their respective states, but what if it's reversed? What if they are actually the prosecutors? What if they burn the fuck out of me for attention, to show how righteous they are to win the undecided voters, the illegals and the Democratic votes? They claim to be righteous Republicans but then again how many Rhinos are in Congress, in the House and all the other political offices? They're everywhere, they're just fucking snakes, snakes that should be beheaded. However beheaded rattlesnakes can still deliver a full dose of venom from their fangs twelve hours after their head is severed. I've got to get away from this shit in my head, this is too crazy making. I don't care for this kind of drama today, maybe at another time. Maybe if I felt better, maybe If I was given an exemption from prosecution for helping bad people disappear, I am sure that I could find an inner strength to carry out the job. But we know that's not going to happen, just another fantasy, how do I get away from these fuckers? I've got to give myself time to think but then do I have the time now? No not currently, I guess I'll just dive into this shit pool without any PPE, snorkel or goggles and see where it goes but I'll be damned if I'll let them lock me down, put me on a schedule and maybe have me perform like a fucking circus bear! I'm still going to hold my power just in a different way perhaps.

      Yes, so I did decide that Phil was the weakest link. Not weak by any means but perhaps more willing, more willing in the integrity and honesty department. I just have to open the door for her. I called Phil on her cell and asked where she was. She said she was meeting with the ladies in Marge's room.

Me: That's swell sweetheart, now you need to take your leave from there, return to your room and wait for a knock on your door, it'll just be a few minutes. Two of my most trusted security agents will escort you up to the Eagles Nest. Bring nothing with you, no notebook, no notepad, no purse, or briefcase. Just bring you and just so you know sweetheart, you will be searched.

I was waiting for Phil and the two security agents in the hallway as the elevator doors opened on the top level. I pulled one of the agents aside and walked him to the far end of the hall and quietly told him what I wanted. He nodded and said he would send it in a secure text as soon as it loaded. I thanked them for their service and said to Phil, "Come with me" as I walked her down the hall and took her through the open doors of the Eagles Nest.

Me: Sweetheart, I'm going to search you now, if you think I'm groping you, it's possible that I may be but I also have to protect myself, thusly the search.

Phil seemed a bit reluctant and yet at the same time somewhat excited. She didn't try to pull away from me but she didn't move forward either. She let me press my hands and fingertips all over her body, top to bottom. I then said, "Baby have a seat, I want to know about you. There's something about you that stands apart from the other two. There's a distinct but well hidden difference. I want to know what that difference is, let's start with where did you come from, how did you meet these two dolls?

Phil: David, we met at college, we all attended Columbia University School of Law. The three of us were put together into a two year study group.

Me: So you and them attended the nation's top ivy league college where it requires a minimum of a 3.7 GPA just to walk in the front door. They've hosted 84 Nobel Prize winners, 90 Pulitzer Prize winners, 4 United States presidents and something like 46 Olympians. How did you get accepted there? Remember to try not to bullshit me, I have people too.

Phil: David, I didn't belong there. My GPA carried me in, but financially I didn't belong there, I was not a, "Silver Spooner." I received a great deal of financial assistance through several different organizations for grants and scholarships. Most students lived on campus, either in dorms or in condos. I couldn't afford either. I didn't even have a car. Parking permits were $1,200 a month for campus parking and $450 a month for apartment parking. I rented a third story studio apartment six miles from campus. There wasn't much room but then again I didn't need much room. I rode the bus each day to school and some days it was frightening, especially when I had late night studies. The area where I lived was not a safe area.

Me: Okay great, so you're a poor kid from some part of the country and it's really not important where that was. You pushed your way into one of the most prestigious colleges in the world and became a lawyer. How cute, now there's a lovely success story and of late, you have been studying me. I don't mean the kind of study like reading my books, I mean the kind of study where you look at me differently than the other two women do. I think I know what's behind it so you better bring it up and bring it out babes.

   I waved off Phil as I heard my cell phone beep with a priority message alert. The secured text came up on my phone. It was a video along with several close-up frame by frame still photos. It was as I suspected. I nodded to Phil to continue.

   Phil: Well David, I've known about you for a very long time. There was a woman that lived in my same building that I would see on a regular basis. She noticed me waiting for the bus one morning and she stopped her car and asked me where I was going? I said, "Columbia School of Law." She said, "Ride with me, I'm going there too but I'm going to the Department of Psychiatry." It turns out that she and I have become close and trusted friends. Her name is Amy. Before the day she gave me a ride, we bumped into each other a couple times in the community laundry room of our complex. Going to the laundry room was scary at night, so we made a pact that we would let each other know when we're going to do our laundry. We would go there together to be safe, she gave me a ride to school everyday and oftentimes Amy would even study in the library and wait for me to get out of class so she could give me a ride home. Early in our friendship, Amy talked of her dream man who was an undiscovered and greatly unappreciated novelist. David, she was talking about you, she was crazy about you, you were her absent lover.

    She was studying psychology and she wanted to be a psychologist and she wanted to work with damaged people who came from the first responder communities. She thought that you had the best finger on the pulse of anyone and she always thought it was sad that you were so under-educated and underappreciated. Amy turned me on to your writings. I Facebook friend requested you using a fictitious name and city. I wanted to study you. You have an incredible sense of humor that goes along with but not quite matches the tragic things that you write about in your books. I was astounded to find that you were a writer and of course I read your first book, several times over. I was always hoping that you'd write another book, then suddenly on Facebook, you posted that you've written another and then you wrote another and another and another and I couldn't get enough of any of them. Amy and I would discuss you often, almost daily as a matter of fact. Amy would tell me that you've taught her more about mental health and the way the human mind works more than most any instructors would, because you draw from your own true life experience. They only draw from what they've been taught. Few people have that level of courage to investigate themselves. I have to be honest with you about something, I so very thoroughly enjoyed you searching me a few minutes ago. I felt your power and your gentleness at the same time. Of course you were feeling for recording wires and microphones. You could teach those clumsy fucking TSA workers how to properly touch a lady. I may have had an orgasm, I'll have to check later. David I attached to you right away in your writings. I have had my personal struggles along with a number of my family members with mental health issues but none of us ever spoke about it, it was our closely guarded family secret. I have searched everything that I possibly could to find out about you, long before I got together with the other two ladies. I was enthralled by you, you are my rock star and believe me when I tell you this, regardless of your current age you are still hot as fuck! You look just like the kind of bad boy that I was hoping to find, hell all women want your image. Your readers fully see you as a man with many benefits, a man with a dirty mind and exquisite dirty talk. There's no excitement which compares to sexual excitement, I've always secretly been that way. Before I found you, I used to shop for bad boys online. I've traveled to Spokane, Las Vegas, Philadelphia and Miami looking to find the perfect bad boy, a bad boy like you! I paid these male, 'escorts' $5,000 for a one-night date but it was never what I hoped it would be. I knew there had to be more, I just didn't know how to reach it. Now, spending this time with you, I've reached it. If it wasn't for your wife Heather, I would lock you down and keep you forever. You excite me just with your look, just the way you move your hands and your eyes, your penetrating liquid green eyes all but stop my heart. So yes, I do look at you differently because you are different. You're more different than any human being I've ever met and I can't get enough of you. I'm protecting the man I love. So of the three of us ladies, I am the most dogmatic in your matter.

    Me: Slow your roll baby. Your credibility is losing its shine by the second. You just said, "If it wasn't for Heather that you would lock me down and keep me forever." Would you like me to play the tape back for you? Yes darling, every room on this entire floor is bugged. Remember sweetie that this is my ballpark that you and your chums are playing in. You are quite photogenic by the way. Look here babes, after I called you to go to your room, you stepped out of Doris's room wearing sweatpants, an oversized football jersey and flip flops. Your hair was pulled back into a ponytail with a purple scrunchie. You did not have any makeup or lip gloss on. When you answered the door for your security escort just a few minutes later, your hair was brushed nicely, with a large black and white polka-dot bow with trailing ribbons, and this cute little short sundress that gets several high school kids married long before they want to. You came here in the hopes of getting laid. I especially enjoyed the way you brought the straps of your dress off your shoulders down to your arms and adjusted your breasts, as I was talking to my security agent. Beyond that, you are setting yourself up to slip behind Heather to push her over the cliff. Any arguments?

    Phil: David, my superpower is to admit that I'm caught when I sense there are multiple landmines

all around me. That doesn't happen to me very often, you are very crafty in the way you set people up. You are the ultimate of all apex predators on all levels. You don't try to match wits with anyone, you simply out-smart them long before they realize that they already lost. So my dearest, I plead guilty. If ever the day should come when you are available, I will fight anyone that tries to take you from me!
    Me: I believe that sweetheart, how do you think you would do going up against my Dementia?
    Phil sat wide eyed for a few moments and then suddenly gushed into tears.
I set a box of kleenex in front of her and put the afghan over her shoulders that was on the couch behind her. I unequivocally knew that she was in love with me and I knew that I had to escape immediately. I lifted her chin with my curled pointer finger and said, "Get out of your gut and get into your head and stay there. You are a professional, not a homewrecker or a hooker. Security will be here in a few minutes to escort you to your room where you will put on the very same clothes that you were wearing in Doris's room. You will then be brought back here to wait for me.

    I bolted from the room and called Tim during the elevator ride.

    Me: Timmy me lad, where are you?
    Tim: I am hand waxing your Maserati you asshole. I'm in the security office watching a loop tape

of a super hottie leaving her room to go to yours. I hope you two didn't stain the couch.

    Me: Cute you dick head, meet me in the lobby, I need you to walk with me.

    Tim: You need 'the noise'? Maybe you should stop pissing everyone off and see if that works?

    Me: No dink, I need to walk and I need a spotter to help me not fall on my ass.

    Tim: Okay boss, noise for one, see you in a minute.

I told Tim that I just needed to first clear my mind so I can think properly again. Tim got it and didnt say a word during our walk, nether did I. As we were about to enter the hotel Tim lightly tugged on my shirt sleeve and said, "You do know that I was just fucking with you with my, 'not staining the couch' comment, right? I know that you would never do that with anyone but your lady, Heather.

    Me: We are good buddy, you know me too well. Need me to tell those dolls that you need another twenty grand?

Chapter 7
The Great Insurrection

I knew that I had to get this train back on the tracks. At the same time I had to wonder if the sobbing lady upstairs was playing me. Was it all an act to see If I was as loyal and honorable as I acted? Was she searching for my weaknesses using her beauty and body as a litmus test? Admittedly, it was a passing thought. This will be the last time I meet with any of these dolls on a one on one, that's for damn sure!

Me: You recovered well young lady, it's nice to see you with a clean face again. I am not going to challenge you with what part of that act was real and what wasn't. It's not important, what is important is that you must understand that I have my limits and you came very close to stepping over that line. I don't want that to happen again with you or them. Now tell me babes, what's your relationship with these other two women outside of your claiming you're burning desires for Governor's chairs, what do those other two think of you

    Phil: They admire my drive but they don't know what's behind that drive and they're never going to. I love you David, I've been in love with you for a very long time and when I sit with you, as I am now, I find hope for myself and I want to promise you within my heart of hearts, that I will not let you fall, no one is going to take you down, if they do it'll have to be in a hail of gunfire and I'll lay on top of you as cover, as I return fire.

    Me: Well honey, remind me to send your dear friend Amy a Christmas card, would you please? Look sweetheart, you're a smart girl. I am not a mind reader, not the fixer of broken brains or shattered hearts. I'm just a man that admitted his truths for his own wellness. I don't have anything for you baby. Yes, I was looking for wires but don't think for a moment that I didn't enjoy touching you where I touched you, and no I didn't linger in any one particular spot but I absorbed it if you know what I mean. So what we're talking about here sweetheart are fantasies. The reason of course why they're called fantasies is because we know they're never going to be within our reach. Dreams yes, fantasies no. I find that I can only speak of myself. When I entertain a fantasy, it's because I'm not okay with what's going on in my life at that moment. You might find this strange, perhaps even entertaining, hell maybe you could even write and publish a paper on it, who knows? When I was single, I interviewed every female before I ever touched her because I wanted to know what she was about. Oh believe me, it didn't take long, I could do that in under 15 minutes. I would get right to it, people waste their time and money on bullshit high dollar flowers, chocolates, dinners, drinks, dancing, the theater, as well as paying for a babysitter and all that other courtship bullshit. I would casually say to a woman who approached me, "You know what baby, you're a hot looking chick, it's more than a bit obvious that you're of the same thoughts with me, what do you say we fuck? If not, you need to be on your way. I would ask a woman where their G-spot was. It's just ridiculous how men play this searching game and women play this hide and seek game of, "Try to find my G-spot, I'll let you know if you do..... maybe."

There is an old golfers joke that isn't all that funny. It goes something like, "A man will look for his lost golf ball in the wood tic and snake infested tall grass for an hour, yet when he gets home he will spend less than three minutes looking for his woman's G-spot."

There is a lot of sad truth in that joke. That's fucking nonsense, what a waste of time. If a man or woman can't be honest about their sexual likes and dislikes then they can't be honest about anything else in their relationship either. What's the number one reason why couples step out of the relationship, why do they cheat? It's really simple, their needs aren't being met. Now let's take that apart and ask what needs she or he may say they are lacking? Chances are that they don't even know what they're fucking (pun intended) needs are. They just know they need something different. Well there's some insanity right there. They risk their security of their relationship or marriage, their home and everything else they currently have, for what?

    I'll give you a tragic and ugly example. I have a close friend that married a good gal but a wrong girl, wrong for him at least. She became someone she never was before once she had him locked down. He was all in, heart, dreams and money. She played the cute game from the beginning but as time went on, she became more and more assertive. Once she knew she had him deep in his heart, she became who she actually was all along. Suddenly they have strong political disagreements, suddenly he put the wrong thing in the wrong location in the dishwasher, suddenly he doesn't know how to mop a floor any longer, suddenly he doesn't know how to do laundry properly and this continued on and on and on until one fine day when she had him served with divorce papers. She was punishing him for failing to satisfy her never spoken of needs! I may have failed to mention that she suddenly had to work late at night, had business meeting dinners with clients and several out of state multiple day business trips, which seemed to coincide with her starting to find fault with everything he did. He continued to bow to her but it was never enough, it was never enough because she realized she didn't want him anymore. He couldn't do anything right, because nothing about him was right for her. Well she had the strength to break away and go out on her own and never looked back. He had no choice, his options were non-existent, he offered to go to marriage counseling, he even said he would move out for the summer to give her her space with the hopes of having a weekly date. He was met with a resounding, no! He loved her, she saw him as only a meal ticket.

    So what does he do after she takes all the furniture, drained the bank accounts and leaves all the bills as she walks out? He isolated and plunged into severe depression and dove into the 'stupid pool' and currently hides out in YouTube land. He didn't engage with anyone, he kept to himself and locked the door on life and society. He had always been a private kind of guy and had only a few social skills. Oh he was a perfect gentleman without question, but as far as relationships, he'd had some bad fortune in his past. He had some terribly bad fortune, the word fortune doesn't even belong in there but he's now recovering slowly. He's gotten involved in things that interest him because you see he was lonely and he was willing to sell his soul to not be alone. He still hasn't been willing to admit that he settled because he was simply lonely. People settle for the most ridiculous reasons, "Oh he or she has a good job." "Yeah I want to get up with him or her because they own a nice house." "I want to get up with him or her with this or that or this" or that and people will say, "Well I can overlook that little one thing or those few other little things."

Those little things become huge fucking things, they become unclimbable mountains after a period of time. Why, because again our fantasies weren't fulfilled by this person as we thought they would be so now what do we do? We punish them by withholding sweet smiles, kind words, affection and of course intimacy. Men and women both do it. We punish our mate or our partner because our needs aren't being met and oftentimes we punish people hoping that they will get the hint and just go away. When they don't go away, we go away whether that be a divorce or again stepping out of the relationship and just flat out embrace cheating as if it's some kind of sport. I hope that I've lined out this whole fantasy thing for you honey. Fantasies don't work, they're fun, they're an escape but what drives them oftentimes is a deep loneliness. So I'm going to give you ten minutes and you can tell me all about your womanhood. I don't care about your childhood, I don't care anything about your family and your upbringing. I want to know about you, the person that's sitting here at this very moment.

Phil: David there you go again, how in the hell do you make things so clear and concise? It just rolls off your tongue with the thoughts of thousands of men and women who could never admit to having those thoughts or even identify what's behind those thoughts. You just puke it out like you ate some bad Sushi or something! How in the fuck do you do that mister? You've had no professional training, oh you've had some training all right and it all came from your own mistakes within your life but look at how you become someone who no one thought you could ever be. Perhaps you yourself didn't even think you could be? David, I don't know how to help you understand that in the grand scheme of life, that you have arrived! You've won, you're the king of the world and I don't think you actually understand that.

    Me: Well that's wonderful sweetheart but you know what babe, I still drive a 22-year-old pickup truck, I still live on my Social Security and my very few book sales, if it wasn't for Heather supporting us I'd probably starve to death or freeze to death or however else you die when you have no financial support of any kind. Yes I'm blessed, I'm blessed to be with Heather, I'm blessed in fact that she does love me and we're buddies, you know, speaking of Heather I have to tell you what she has told this friend I just mentioned to you a few minutes ago. She has advised him that he needs to make friends with a woman first, rather than just try to get his dick wet. He needs to make friends that turn in the best friends before he should ever consider them as a lover or a life mate. Well that's really swell and all but it's not the way I see it. But you know what? Heather does have some valid points, none of which I would ever entertain because well, I'm a filthy pick. So yeah, I have no magical secrets and I have no special formula. I'm just a guy, I'm just a guy that had a spiritual experience that told me I needed to write a book and from there it was a whole thing of self-discovery and of course, I recorded it in book form. And now honey, I have to tell you that I too shake my head often when I go to my back bedroom and I look at the large dresser top in the bedroom that I don't want anyone sleeping in. On top of the large dresser are all of my books in plexiglass display book holders. When I walk down the hall and see it, I'm almost directed, hell I'm almost pulled into the doorway of that room and I'll stand there with my arms at my side and just look at all my books with thinking, "This is all a gift, this is God's work, this is truly my blessing, this is my calling" and the tears follow. Tears of gratitude and the joy of freedom.

    Now I want to get back to what you're doing here. Okay why me, why all this Cloak and Dagger shit? Can you people be trusted, are you batting for the other side? These are questions I ask myself, questions I have to ask you. I have seen the filthiness of politics, we all have as a nation and it sickens me, I hope it sickens you too. No matter what party we vote within, how do we know if our votes are even counted. Even the most left sided democrats know that our current president could not have possibly won that election with eighty million votes, he wasn't elected into office, he was installed, installed like a fuckin toilet!

    I need you to trust me so I can trust you. I don't know how I'll know, so I'll need you to convince me, are you truly working for me? Am I your only true purpose for being here? Yeah I get that whole thing about you girls running for governor and I'm all for it and I truly hope that happens, I'll do all I can to help but for now I'm only going to talk with you dolls about my freedom, about me not being put away. So yeah, I got a dog in this fight. I just hope it's a big enough dog. So now my darling child, tell me about you, the current you.

    Phil: David I did it like everyone else does, not that it's a reason or an excuse. I find sex to be unfulfilling, I find romance to be unfulfilling, I find friendships to be unfulfilling and I'm sure it has everything to do with my expectations and nothing to do with my reality. I've been married only once to a very nice guy and I guess you could say we were friends as far as you could take a friendship. We had sex often but we were never lovers. We didn't care about each other with the deepest of all passions, it wasn't like that for me and I believe it wasn't that for him. I got married because, well that's what you're supposed to do. Of course there was family pressure that I didn't have to bow to but I chose to for acceptance like most others and you laid that whole thing out for me already. I carried a fantasy that I would become a powerful woman, a leader of people and not just women because I don't like that bullshit of, "I'm a woman so I'm strictly just for all woman things." I don't operate like that, our marriage didn't have a chance. I didn't know how to be a partner nor did he but that's his deal not mine. I'm not going to cast any aspersions upon him as to what he was but he wasn't what I wanted and I of course with my dishonesty wasn't what he wanted and that's emotional dishonesty by the way. I never stepped out of the relationship, we just drifted apart. We pretty much shook hands, wished each other well and we both went our separate ways. I didn't need his money for support, I didn't need to attack and rape him for his possessions and property. I didn't have anything to get even with him for. I didn't want to punish him, there was no need for that nonsense. I just knew that I wasn't happy and I knew I couldn't live in my lies any longer. So we had a very amicable divorce. We even went out for dinner a few times afterwards. Then he went off to find his life and I to find mine. So here I sit today, I'm hard driven, I have ambition and the wherewithal and the means to be successful. I am financially secure and unafraid but yes, I lack, I greatly lack a true loving relationship. I would give everything up to have a man like you.

    Me: So I guess you're saying if Heather and I don't work out that you're next in line, is that what you're telling me? You think that you got first dibs on me? Baby you are like most any other woman that's been in my life and that's not a negative thing it's just a simple fact. The fact is that I will never be what's considered a whole man. I'm a functional man but not a whole man and the greatest downside of all of that is I can never find my own peace. It just is not in the cards for me and I know it. Again, not only have I had five wonderful wives I've also had other women in my life as well. They all made that one same mistake, they all thought they could make the difference. They thought that they could change me, they thought they could heal me and make me whole. I'm sure I played a role in that, women look at me as a project like I'm a

THE GHOST IN OUR LOCKERS

Mr. Potato Head or a Build-A-Bear, maybe even more like a few cans of Play-Doh, where they can just shape and mold anything they want. As you can see, none of that worked for any of them. I disappointed each and every one of those women. At the time I was unaware of my effect on them because of my own selfish, needy bastard behaviors.

Let me tell you how I roll. I've lived this way most of my adult life, perhaps even when I was younger. You see, I never liked all the guessing games when I first met a woman. Understand that when I meet a woman I'm not looking for a new best friend. I'm only looking to get laid and I move on afterwards. I didn't like that back and forth coy, cutesy, come get me big boy, crap. That just wasn't me, if in fact I saw a woman that I wanted to bed, my first question would be, "Are you all women? As I reach down and brushed my hand across her crotch looking for a dick, at the same time I was swiping my hand over each breast. If she was still willing to go along I would invite her to a hotel room but never to my place and most certainly never her place. Going to a woman's place would be a transfer of power, I wouldn't allow a woman to one-up me on the first meeting. I would tell her that we would shower together as soon as we got to the room. If she balked in the least, the deal was over. I want to see what she really looked like without makeup. How she handled herself with a man's body pressed against her while his hands were roaming all around her. If she showed any hesitation it would be the last time that I would see her.

So now I'm back to telling you as I've told so many others that my life today is about a simple man, making simple amends to people I've never even met and that is simply about showing acts of kindness. Now we're back to holding the doors for someone whether it be male or female, we're back to the simple head nod of recognition, we're back to the good morning, good afternoon, good evening greetings of total strangers we see on the street or in public places, It's just about being a nice guy and today I am a nice guy, but I do have my limitations. Push me and I'll push back and my push back will be far more greater than anyone that tries to push me. So yeah your question is, "How dangerous are you?" I think that's a fair question I can only answer with, fuck with me and find out.

Admittedly my love, there was a reason I didn't take you into my arms and try to comfort you. Yes, there are moments of my life where I don't even trust myself. I couldn't risk my being trapped. You do however present a mighty fine package of temptation. I don't want to see that again from you or from those other dolls. This is all about business, there is no time for play time or whatever the fuck time you want to call it. This whole deal will be over for me if there is any more of this bullshit, and I will walk. I know how to handle myself in a courtroom. Tell me you understand, now get off my couch and go report to those other two dolls that the games are now officially and forever over! Now run along and tell your little playmates that the fuckery has concluded. I'll meet you three in the restaurant in one hour. Still love me babe?

Chapter 8
Setting The Underpinnings

The ladies were seated before I arrived at the restaurant. The looks on her faces showed me that they now had a clear understanding of what I was about and about what their role is.

Me: Well girls tell me about your last travel trip for pleasure, nothing skanky however.

I quickly learned that those three are in fact, true world travelers. Only one of them liked to go on cruises, the other ones felt cruise ships stole their time, as their playtime was quite short because of their caseloads. So they spent a lot of money on airfare but packed in a lot of pleasure on those short jaunts. There was no conversation at that table about why we were together or the case itself. Yeah they were far too experienced and professional to let anything slip out in public. They knew that they live a fishbowl lifestyle, long before they found me.

I found their demeanor to be attractive all by itself then add the obvious fact that they are smart, beautiful and cunning. Yep, they're the kittie cats, watching the fishbowl without question and I'm sure when the time comes they could bust balls with the best of them, just not my balls!

As we got up from the table I nodded towards the doorway and escorted the ladies to the elevator. We went up to the Eagles Nest and it was time to get to business.

Me: All right ladies, let's get down to it, go ahead and drag out all those easels and place your grease boards on each one of them. You think you want to run this show? Go ahead, I'm going to sit back and see how well you do. Go ahead, give me the layout, what's your strategy? I'm going to go to make some popcorn while you kids set everything up.

I knew that I had been pushing them hard. I've even been mistreating them intentionally trying to show them where the power truly laid but even more importantly, to check their commitment and drive. Hell, I wish I knew where that power was. I'm not feeling it at the moment but I had to stay the course. I still have to fight for my freedom either with or without them, so I knew I had to play nice with these dolls and slow down with the locker room talk. I have to remind myself that they are professionals and they are also ladies.

Me: Ladies I know that as professionals, as highly experienced professionals I may add, that you must understand the all too often overlooked need to build a solid foundation, with any case. In my case we had to drill four and a half feet down into our yard to put in casements for our deck supports. It took a lot of work by the contractors and cost a hell of a lot of money but just like the old trucker will say as he snaps a taunt cargo strap, "This fucker ain't going anywhere!"

    I'm sure that you're more than a bit miffed with how I keep trying to take over the show. Yes it's your show, there's no question about that but it's my theater. I own this theater and I will be the director, so show me what you have and no, you can't have any of my popcorn, go get your own.

    Marge: David, I know that you're fully aware that these bastards will come at you from every angle, side to side, top to bottom and inside out. They will use people, places and things to discredit you, that's what this is truly all about. They can't prove or disprove anything and they don't have to. Their only purpose is to shift blame and public opinion. Once we go into the hearing room, they hold the power, it's their hearing, it's their room, no different than you were just describing your theater. We have to be prepared for anything and everything. We also have three research assistants with us. I would like to bring them in as we start this. I want them to be at full speed as they're given their new assignments, they have been on assignment for the last two weeks.

    Me: That's a swell idea babe, yeah ring those people up and have them stand in the lobby at the registration desk and wait for Tim. Tim will escort them up here.

Of course, I found it quite interesting that there was one female and two males in the group of three. Maybe early to mid 30s, well groomed and well dressed. I had them sit on my side of the sixteen person oblong meeting table. After the introductions of Wyatt, Frederick and Abby, I had to stifle my giggles. Good ole Frederick had to immediately jump in with, "That's Frederic without a 'K' as my name is spelled Frederic." I wanted to tell him how fucking delighted I was for him that he was minus a 'K'. I think that I'll just let that bullshit simmer for a while.

Me: I would like to say it's nice to meet you three but I am going to withhold that nicety until you three can convince me that you are truly nice. I give and use nicknames to most everyone I meet. Wyatt, your name will remain the same but only because I like western history, western books, western movies and western tv shows. Don't get too carried away with all of that sport, I like your name, not you.

For you Frederic, without a 'K', your name is now Fred. I expect you all to refer to Frederic as 'Fred' from this point forward.

For you Abby, your name is now Abs. I once again expect you all to refer to Abby as 'Abs' from this point forward.

Moving on, my life experience tells me everything I need to know about a person in the first few minutes we meet. My unit of measure is eye contact and posture. You three are quite easy to read, even with two of you sitting like you're at a poker table with a pool cue up your ass.

    I glanced over at Doris and asked her if she wouldn't come and sit on this side of the table, "Sit on my side sweetheart, because I'm sure that Marge would like to have her son, Fred sitting next to her." The look on Marge's face, along with the other two, was quite interesting. During all this time, Tim was standing alongside me as I said, "Timmy, I'd like you to have a seat, you're part of this show, ladies you need to bust out another twenty grand for this man. Marge, I would like to sell you a bullshit story about how my man Tim pulled your DNA from the courtesy water bottle in your hotel room trash, to find that this young gent was your son but the truth is, I wasn't sure up until just now. The look on your face a moment ago, gave me that affirmation.
    I don't know who you other two folks are but let me give you all a few ground rules before we start. I don't give a shit about what you think, what you feel or what you identify as. Your pronouns don't fucking matter either. I don't care if you identify as a damned toaster, there is no room for that bullshit here. All I want to know is what you're going to do for me. Now as far as your personal appearance, I don't want to see any facial piercings or jewelry, if you have tongue jewelry get it out! If you have neck tattoos wear a fucking scarf. When it comes to wardrobe, I don't want

to see any male wearing skinny jeans, I don't want to see any female wearing less than they should, your and our professionalism starts here and now, in this room and it will carry us forward until your happy asses are burning gas on your way back home, hoping to never hear my name or see me ever again. Now a little birdie has made mention that you three younger people are not just research assistants, but you are actually all licensed attorneys, licensed in several states in fact and all are in good standing with the Bar Association. My man Tim has found that you three youngsters plan on being lieutenant governors and one of you is demanding that they be the State Attorney General. I have to assume that you Wyatt, wants to be the Attorney General, the top cop of the entire state and since you're aptly named Wyatt as in Wyatt Earp or perhaps you know your name came from your mother as your dad was flopping up and down on top of your mom one fine afternoon and just as your dad was busting his nut, your mother screamed out what your dad thought to be Wyatt but she was really saying was 'wait' meaning that she wasn't done yet! Now have I helped you understand your place at this table?

    Wyatt, I'm sitting here almost feeling sorry for you. When I went over your dossier last night along with some other information that you foolishly thought was well guarded, I found a softness in my heart for you, but don't expect it to last. You see young man, you've never had a chance at life. You were programmed and molded before you were even born.

Your parents selfishly wanted to raise a winner, even at the cost of your own childhood and yes they got their way no question about it. As a young child you went to every Sports Camp and learning center that your parents could possibly inject into you, you were nothing more than a project. You started gathering ribbons, medals, and trophies before you were even five years old. Yes you definitely earned them but at what cost? Looking at some of your childhood x-rays with a radiologist friend of mine, it shows you have had several juvenile stress fractures. Your parents put you into sports programs that didn't allow your young body to properly form. Your growth spurts were painful for you because you were still developing. Your body couldn't take the stress and abuse. In your parents' minds everything about you had to scream winner and champion. Your parents used you to live out their fantasies. Jesus Christ young man, your high school letter jacket had as many ribbons, pins and patches as some of the North Korean generals have. Those silly little fuckers even have medals running down their pants legs! You were nothing but a cyborg to them. To them it was like growing a prize flower or melon or whatever the fuck kind of vegetables people grow for the State Fair. They had to have the blue ribbon even at the cost of your own mental, emotional and physical wellness. So now you sit here today thinking and believing that you are superior to all mankind. Yes your high school and college grades speak of your high level of intelligence but you're one of those guys that's nothing more than garbage in garbage out. I have to question what you retained but here's something that was left out of the whole recipe when building a human being, you have no social skills, You're not well liked, you never were well liked because of your arrogance. You were taught to be arrogant so here's a deal sport, let go of all that bullshit, none of that belongs to you. None of that belongs here in this room today. You are a young professional with a monumental challenge in front of you and you're going to meet that challenge while displaying dignity and warmth. There's no competition here, everyone will have their assignment. There will be no free-wheeling here.

As long as I'm tearing into you people, understand this. Once again, this is my show you can ask me any questions you would like, supposedly for the sake of the case. I will now share with you all, my 'safe word', and that safe word is, 'pass'. My safe word has to do with the only warning you will receive before your ass is dumped out on the street curb. When I say 'pass' I fucking mean it, don't try to come around the back door the side door or any other door. Don't try to rephrase your question to get the answer you think you want to hear. I am viciously direct of which Wyatt just found out. In layman's terms which was aptly coined on November 6th 2020, "Fuck around ....find out!"

As far as your dreams and ambitions, I hope that works out for everyone but I'll give you a brief bit of advice. Don't be an arrogant asshole. If you reach your goals and afterwards you sell-out your respective constituents, someone, perhaps not me, but someone will come for you. I hate fucking rinos and if you see that as a threat I'd like you to know that it is a promise, my personal guarantee that you will be held painfully accountable.

Okay let's move on. Where do we start, anyone have one of those chrome telescopic pointer things in their pocket? Let's get to it!

Doris: Our research assistants have gleaned some very credible and important information, so I propose, (pause) no I'm sorry David. I don't propose, let me restate that, I am going to start with your first book, "Daddy Had To Say Goodbye."

I sat back and loudly clapped my hands while saying, "Doris, you did it right girl, please continue."

Doris: We six all agree that your writing is brilliant and there is no and there can never be a question about your genius. What impresses me and us the most, is how you were able to reach into other people's hearts, according to our stacks of your loyal readers' comments. You mention people's names in your books, you claim them to be fictitious, however we are not convinced of that, not in every case at least. We have to speak to every real character and rule out the others as we are certain the enemy camp has already done that. We must investigate every situation, every condition and every person that we possibly can locate, we can't overlook anything or anyone. Once the ball starts to roll in the hearing room, we can't call for a time out. There is a good chance that they will withhold evidence and deny our request for discovery. Hell David, we're pretty sure that they won't even allow us to object to anything. All I will probably be able to do is to signal you to answer or not to answer. That's going to be our role but for now in this office, we must put together our war plan and we must win this war. It'll be a win for you, a win for us and just as importantly, a win for the American people.

    Me: Sure thing babe as soon as Tim and I get back. We're going to step out and have a brief confab as to whether or not we eat lunch before or after noon. Sit tight for now and everybody please enjoy the show.

    I pressed the remote which opened the floor to ceiling drapes. The three newcomers all but gasped at the view as I said, "Hey kids, give me a few minutes, I've got to wash these windows, they look kind of dusty, as I pushed another button on the remote and a squeegee was spraying soapy water that went up and down the full length of the windows, each window had those installed. The look on their faces of absolute astonishment was quite interesting, so I pushed the third button as I said, "Kids if you want to step out for a taste of fresh air and sun, watch this." I pressed the 3rd button and two of the windows slid open and out popped a railing sun deck. "We're 18 stories high, don't worry if you fall, we have a superb ground crew that will clean that mess up in no time at all, like it never even happened, enjoy the view"

Tim and I giggled during the elevator ride.

Tim: I love the way you went after Wyatt, yeah he's a pompous little prick, I think you shut him and them down, like you always say, 'fast, hard and dirty'. You, my friend, are the man! That thing you said about ground maintenance cleaning up the mess in case someone fell the eighteen stories, gave them all immediate ghost faces.

Me: I'm not too sure about me being the man these days. Tim I want you to be involved with this deal Tim because I'm not the man, at least I'm not the man I once was just a few short months back. I'll need backup, you're the only one I trust in that entire room, hell, in this entire building! I'm still not sold on what they're true purpose of being here is. You and I need a safe word so either you can redirect me or remove me from the room before I trip on my own dick. So let's go back inside and let the games begin.

Tim: I got you buddy let's do this thing, let's use your dog, Gibbs name.

Me: Okay pal, Gibbs it is.

We walked into the Eagles Nest and saw the six of them standing at a respectful and safe distance from the open windows.

Me: Anyone venture out to enjoy the view from the sun deck?

I suspect at least a few had a queasy tummy.

Me: Folks I hope you enjoyed the view because I'm going to close the windows, retract the deck and draw the drapes, so we can focus on what we're here for. I'm sure the strategies in your minds are absolutely foolproof. Well kids, I have a strategy as well. When we get to the hearing or trial or wherever the fuck you want to call it, I personally am going to speak. I'm going to give my opening statement, let me emphasize, "My opening statement" which will be rather brief. I'm going to request that I not be addressed as "Mr. Brown" I will be addressed as, "Victim Brown" because this is not only ridiculous and against any law of the land, hell you may as well just set our constitution on fire. That's what you all have already done and in all actuality, all you have to do now is to sweep up the ashes!"

Okay kids who's first? First question please and yes, you assistant people may ask questions as well.

Abby: David, it is not entirely clear and it's not stated anywhere in your very first book, "Daddy Had To Say Goodbye." But are you in fact the character, Clinton Flanagan?

Me: Good question Abs, before I answer I must ask you this. Would you like me to be Clinton Flanagan?

Abby: You do match the physical description of course but you show no signs of being severely damaged with the marrow deep pain as you describe your character, Clinton Flanagan.

Me: Abs, I strongly advise that you stay with law because your knowledge of the human endeavor is greatly lacking. In truth my dear, you suck at it! Yes honey, I am the character Clintion Flanagan, again all of my books are my true life story. Only locations and names are fictitious but the story is gut punching real.

Abby: David, your opening sentence has only nine words and you set the entire stage of not just the main character but the entire 334 page book! You write, "Clinton Flanagan stood as he lived, rigid and alone." That is gut-wrenching and heartbreaking. It screams of loneliness and you take it right up to having the stoic posture of a Marine and the gentleness of a Priest. That just set me back on my ass.

Me: I'm glad to hear that. That was the desired effect but honey we can't sit here and take this whole fuckin book apart line by line. Keep in mind that we're here to identify what our attackers plan on using as their strategy. They can't attack emotions. If they do, they'll lose their trump card (see what I did there kids, cute huh?) You guys need to sell the teary eye stuff, they will attempt to attack the actions.

Abby: Just so I understand David, your parents had both passed as well as your two brothers before you ever wrote anything, am I correct with that?

Me: Yes my love you are correct in that, my mother's death was the last of those four to pass. My mother's death is what propelled me forward, it's as though her dying gave me permission and license to tell the truth. At no time did I attack them, I explained them and I hope I did them justice, opinions may vary. If not, well who cares they're all dead. Okay Abs, that's enough for now. We're going to move on to someone else's questions. Fred, what have you got?

Frederic: David my mind still hasn't wrapped itself around the kind of life you had to live as a child and the opposition is trying to paint you as a potential serial killer. As I read your books, it all but makes sense, it almost gives you permission to be a serial killer. You have been fucked with and fucked over your entire life. I can't even come close to understanding your level of justifiable rage. At some point in your life you become the ultimate warrior but a tender hearted warrior which makes no sense to me at all.

Me: Well Fred, here's the deal, I was given the opportunity to change my life entirely or perish. I took the easy way out, which always wasn't the easy way. I changed, I changed my attitude and I changed my behaviors all for the price of free. All I had to do was surrender and ask the God of my understanding for guidance. The power of Alcoholics Anonymous is never ending and it has carried people through their entire lives, people like me, who today live free.

Frederic: I just have one other observation, several actually but just one for now. When respect was given, you gave respect, when mercy was necessary you showed mercy but when you were met with violence you became a completely different person. You met violence with extreme prejudice and gave hard and even cruel lessons in what violence is. I'm no sissy but just your writing scared the shit out of me. Now sitting here with you today, it drives that fear even deeper. So I'm vacillating with how do I not fear you and how do I respect you? How do I ask you the hard and dangerous questions without fearing retribution? Can you help me with that?

Me: Yeah buddy, we're back to that same statement of January 6th 2020, "Fuck around….find out!"

Chapter 9
Hard Landing

Okay let's get to the characters. Everything else is subject to speculation, let's stay with the characters and move forward. We have eight books to go through and I don't have the time to play patty-cake. I am not in the best of health and I need to rest and no one's going to drive me into the fucking ground. No one other than me, I may be weakened but I still have purpose and that purpose belongs to me and no one else! *Capiche?*

No disrespect to anyone but as long as we're hearing from your underlings if you will or if you won't, I don't give a fuck. Wyatt, where are you in your head and no, I will not apologize for the spanking I just gave you. I don't like the way you hold yourself, You sit there like you're in a plush leather chair in a fucking, "Members Only" Cigar Bar smoking the finest of the finest cigars as you swish your leaded crystal glass like you're somewhere in fucking France at an invitation only wine tasting. I'm guessing that you may have been the one to finance this little sojourn that you're all enjoying. All that shits going away and that's going away now. Once again, keep this in mind, in the very front of each of your minds. I don't need any of you. Wyatt, the way you set your jaw as if your approval is necessary is how you show your fear, stay away from the poker tables. Buddy it's okay if you're nervous, I understand that, but you're trying to compensate with your posturing isn't going to fly with me. Be you, do you and we'll get along just fine. So let's have it buddy, besides you hating my guts, what question would you like to ask me?

    Wyatt: Well I believe the first character that they are going to use (if in fact he's actually a character or a real person) would be that elderly gentleman named Ivan that you tended to in the ambulance on the way to Minneapolis or was that St. Paul, St, Paul I guess for a brain scan. You admitted to turning off and removing his oxygen mask, giving him a cigarette and when he was done you put the oxygen mask back on him. That's a lot of fodder for the opposing team. If I'm thinking right, they're going to say that you denied him his life supporting oxygen. They're going to say that you did something to his IV. You wrote that he told you that he was ready to meet his maker. They're going to claim that you sent him to meet his maker, afterall he did die while in your care.

    The understanding and tenderness you showed Ivan with your placing that infant in his arms will be ignored, if not be made fun of. I'm only saying these things to better prepare you. David if someone accuses me of that kind of bullshit I'd lose my fucking mind!

    Me: Wyatt, now I'm starting to like you. Yeah I get that, no he didn't have an IV and I don't know if the autopsy showed any fresh injection sites but I'm sure that they'll play with that too but no, I didn't kill that sweet old man. I held his hand as he died and yes I wept, okay who's next?

    Doris: David, chapter #14, "My Blue Baby" brought an emotion that I haven't allowed in my heart to come forward for many, many years. I lost an infant child to 'Sudden Infant Death Syndrome'. If anyone challenges whether or not you have a heart or you as a professional paramedic they will lose in that category. With you and that infant baby and then with you stepping outside of the ER and looking into the predawn sky whispering to your deceased baby daughter Saundra, that "Daddy did this for you." That story all but brought me to my knees, that again is a testimonial as to your sensitivity and loving heart. Of course we then move on to chapter #15 with, "Daddy's Little Buddy." Again, it showed extreme compassion in the way you held the father as he was holding his deceased child and the way you comforted him by your putting a blanket over his shoulders for comfort and privacy and you sitting on the ground behind him, sliding up to him like two little kids on a snow sled and you held him as he rocked back and forth with his dead baby in his arms until the corner arrived. Then your putting Daddy in the back of the ambulance with his son in his arms and you riding up front with your partner shows your kindness and the understanding that you knew that the father needed some time alone with just him and his baby. That was something that I don't even have words for. It was almost as though you were God driven at that moment and as you have alluded to, I think you've been God driven all of your life. I believe it came into truly being when you started to write. Of course you know where this is going David, with you and the baby's daddy and suddenly he was found deceased in the woods with a hunting rifle in his hands.

    I can see where the opposition will make aspersions as to your recklessness with you intentionally ignoring medical and legal protocol with you not securing the baby's body as evidence. They will move on to you pulling the trigger after making a deal with the dad that you would help him end his life. These asshat's will pounce on everything to make you look bad, that's pretty clear to me and I'm sure it is to you. Speaking of that, your ambulance partner Kenny is one of the people we couldn't locate. You've already stated that everything is true in your writing. So Kenny was a real person, correct?

    Me: Yes, Kenny was a real person, not his real name but yes a real person, all of those ambulance incidents took place as I wrote them. As far as you attempting to reach Kenny, Kenny is beyond anyone's reach. As I wrote earlier, Kenny was Native American from a tribe in central Wisconsin. He grew up in a reservation, left the reservation and was terribly ostracized for living like an apple, 'apple' as in red on the outside white on the inside. Racism is just not a white thing. He had a horseshit marriage to a crude and nasty native woman, they had two kids. Kenny always wanted to be a doctor but nobody would fund him because he was an Indian. How would you like to deal with that kind of bullshit kids? As I understand it and this is very common within tribal Indians that when they become sick they return to their home tribe to heal. That wasn't the way it went down for Kenny however. Kenny was found in his apartment on the reservation in a bathtub full of water, he had slashed both his wrists and bled out. No, I wasn't there. No, I never suggested he do that to himself. Hell I hadn't seen Kenny for 50 years or more but it's a sad story. I really dug the guy, he was smart as hell and he was also pretty sensitive to all people. His sense of humor was a little sideways (much like my own) but I dug the guy, we were Pals.

    Phil: David, all throughout your writings the one thing I hear more than anything is your willingness to display your vulnerabilities. That is such a powerful gift, you just lay it all out for everyone to see with no fear of repercussion, you define the word brave. Your level of bravery is to be applauded if not modeled after. I wish there were more David Brown's in this world.

    Me: Thank you honey, now do you have a question.

    Phil: I'm not sure if it's a valid question, I'm just so enthralled with you and your writings. So your mother was of course real, your father was of course real, his cancer was real. I have to assume your mother taking him for Lateral treatments in Mexico had to be terrifying for her. I almost understand where your strength comes from, you've been giving some beautiful examples of what real love is and now that we're talking about what real love is, I would like you to talk about your five wives.

Me: What is this 'we' stuff? I never mentioned anything about 'real love', that was all you. Your question is more than a bit out of sequence, but I get it, so yes I have been married and divorced five times. I have also had relationships with other women between marriages, on a number of occasions even during each of those marriages.

Phil: I guess I first have to know about your first wife, Paula. Are you okay with that?

Me: Yes honey, it's all part of my life story, whether I'm okay with it or not. What's your question?

Phil: In your seventh book you wrote that Paula had passed but it was very clear to me that you still loved her deeply. Had you seen her from the time of your divorce up until the time of her death?

Me: Finally a fucking question! Stop being so fucking placating, I promise that I won't eat your liver. Well, you'll probably find this interesting because she can't be interviewed, there's no harm, no foul in your question.

I ran into Paula about ten years after we were divorced, it was in a tourist restaurant bar in Canal Park. That place wasn't even open when she and I were together. Remember that I was only 17 years old, she was 18 when we were married but yes, ten years later she was at that restaurant. I was sitting at the bar which overlooks the dining areas. A waitress handed me a drink and said it's from the lady from across the room and there sat Paula. She was as gorgeous as ever, maybe even prettier than I can remember.

    Well I knew I had to talk with her, I just couldn't get my feet to work to walk up to her table and I hadn't even had two beers. Paula was sitting with a female and I don't recall her name. We exchanged a few pleasantries. I could see that they were still eating their meal so I invited her to come to the bar when she finished her meal with her friend. Well, I couldn't take my eyes off of her, I couldn't even control my breathing, and yes, I still loved her then as I do today. I watched Paula and her friend rise from the table, hug each other and wave goodbye. Paula walked up to me as she said, "Hey baby, I need a ride home, could you help a gal out?" I almost fell off of my bar stool. I said, "Sure I will!" She said, "Great let's go somewhere and spend some time alone before you give me that ride I need." As we were driving Paula told me that she now lived in Florida and was remarried to an okay guy. He was an Air Force career guy. I don't know what his rank was or what his assignment was. She said she had two children. She went on to say that she was as happy with life as she could possibly be considering her lifelong heartache of losing our baby. I reached over and took her hand and continued to drive, in just a few miles I turned off the highway onto a dirt road. It was an area that I was familiar with, an area where I did a lot of trout fishing a few years back. I led her down a well used game trail that I knew came out to a small meadow. We laid in the center of that meadow holding each other, we both cried and then we made love. As we stood to leave the area and return to the car, a doe deer and her spotted young fawn stepped out into the meadow. We just stood together holding hands watching the deer as they watched us. Paula whispered, "Sweetheart, that Mama dear came to show us her baby because she knows that we never got to hold ours."

I drove her to her parents house, got out of the car and walked her to the door, we had a firm embrace. I gave her a brotherly kiss on her forehead, told her I loved her and told her, "I will see you on the other side someday and the three of us will be reunited."

Tim, get me the fuck out of here!

I got up from my chair with Tims help. We walked out and walked around the block a few times. We both openly shared some tears. I guess I didn't realize just how brutal this session was going to be and how brutal the next several weeks or months or whenever the fuck when. Holy Christ, I thought my brain was going to kill me, maybe now it's my heart that's going to kill me, maybe that's the whole end game? Maybe these fuckers are so filthy that they want to give me a goddamn heart attack, slamming my entire life of failure, heartache and loneliness into one big fucking sack and shoving it right down my fuckin throat!

It was time to return back to the Eagles Nest. I found it interesting that there was a box of Kleenex at every position on that table for each person. Well if there's a jury for this court thing, I'll be more than happy to buy a few cases of Kleenex for them.

Me: Okay you guys, I am going to sit at the end of this table so I can see all of your bright smiling faces, please turn your chairs to face me. We've got to keep this moving. Who's up?

Doris: David, thank you for leaving the room to give us our time. My God, I don't know how any man could stand up to that and not become a blithering idiot for their entire lifetime. I'd like to ask you about Liz. Now is Liz alive today?

Me: Yes she is, as a matter of fact. As I understand it, she lives within twenty-five miles of me. I have not seen her or had any communication with her from the last day I saw her in divorce court. I have a friend who is a pleasure sailor and he has told me over the years that Liz and her husband are avid pleasure sailors and he sees them quite often on different sailing meetups or whatever the fuck they call them. Regadas maybe, I'm not sure. My friend mentioned on several occasions that both her and her husband seemed quite intoxicated, well who knows, I don't give a shit. I have no idea if she has children, if she works or where she works. I know nothing about her and you know what, I'm really cool with that.

There are things with each of those five women that I was married to that happened that are not very attractive. I chose loose women with my thinking that I was all they would ever need. I was under the impression that they would stop being so loose once we were together, well silly ole me! The only thing I have to put out about Liz is that she was the second wife that was adopted. Both of my first and second wives were adopted. I don't have some kind of internal radar that tells me, "Hey there's an adopted gal, she's really going to be a lot of fun." You see, I was not grounded in any way, shape or form, emotionally, mentally or spiritually. I was a fucking mess but I looked good and I thought my looks would gave me what I thought I was after. Today I realized that I was no prize for any of those gals, they all deserved better, I'm not going to sit here and break them down and tell you what bitches and whores they were because that's not true. I can (but won't) tell you how terribly broken they were within themselves. Yes, I may have been the ultimate predator in every one of those situations because when you're a predator, you don't have to be concerned for their well being, you just consume them and go on your way.

Doris: The opposition will have a ball with that one, won't they David? I don't think we'll make mention of that! David, you are so interesting in the way you think and speak. You are more than two dimensional, I can't even count the dimensions you present and no, it's not anything like dual personalities, it's, it's your many emotional tiers of structures and maybe we want to bring in a psychologist. That's your call as a part of your defense if you choose. I don't know at this point but knowing what your mother did to you and how it paralyzed you emotionally for most of your adult life, you might want to visit with a mental health professional for your own wellness.

    Yet when that ambulance call came in for a woman who had fallen and was bleeding from the back of her head we all saw your true colors. That was your mother you tended to, your mother called you several terrible names and fought with you. You had to wrestle with your own mother on the floor of her home and had to handcuff her to care for her and to get her to the hospital for the care she needed. That is heartbreaking and mind-boggling. Whoever has had that thought that they're going to have to fight their own mother to try to save her life, with full well knowing that she will never speak to or see you ever again. That speaks highly of your depth of love for your mother and for all the other people. All of your writing speaks of that unknown and uncommon depth of love you have for all of mankind.

    Me: Okay, yeah swell, this is becoming exhausting, let's stay with characters whether or not they're real can we do that please? Who's got the ball now? Abs I'm giving you the ball, what's in your head babe?

    Abby: David, I would like to ask you about Sandy. Is she still with us today?

    Me: No honey, she had a stroke three years ago. She lingered for about four months before she died. So rather than you ask, I'll just tell you, even after the divorce Sandy was still my buddy. We were always pals right up to her having the stroke. We knew we loved each other but we both knew we weren't right for each other. As a matter of fact, after our divorce we would talk on the phone often. We would meet for drinks often and sometimes we did the nasty together. One day she asked if we could meet for a beer. My answer of course was yes. I met her at a bar and she told me about a guy that she's kind of taken up with. She thinks she might even want to marry him, he's got a nasty vicious ex-wife and has one daughter that his wife uses as a pawn to extract whatever the fuck power she needed to feel.

    Well, her and this fella got married and they moved to a small town in rural Nevada. Sandy and I were Facebook friends, we still talked on the phone maybe once or twice a month and shared emails on a regular basis. Well poor Sandy couldn't ever get away from under herself, meaning that she was broken, no different than I was. She made some, let me say, "extremely dangerous choices" in that marriage but somehow they stayed together. Well they lived in Nevada for, gosh I don't know, 20 years maybe. I had an occasion to be in Las Vegas on a book signing tour. I had contacted her before I ever entertained the idea of going on the tour. When I was in Las Vegas we made plans for her and I and her husband to meet. Her husband became quite ill with cancer a few years back and she was caring for him plus working full time. So I rented a car and drove to their home and when she came out the front door to greet me, my heart sank. She didn't weigh more than a hundred pounds if that, she was absolutely emaciated and looked exhausted. The care that she was providing for her husband was more than just a full time deal. He had to be fed with a feeding tube, she had to prepare all of his food stuff as well as feed him.

    It was quite apparent to me at the time that I'm going to have to outlive this one too. Yeah that was very sad to see her in that condition and that was the last time I saw her. We did get to make amends to each other without admitting all of our faults of course, so we got to make general amends and we both knew that we meant it. We both knew that we still loved each other and most importantly we also knew that we couldn't live together.

    Abby: So your next wife was named Karen?

    Me: Yes that was her name and I'm not going to make mention of anything about her. Yes she claims that she bore us our son. For me however, I've always wondered if that's truly the case and I won't go any further with it. If your people or the opposition contact her for a statement, believe me that you or they won't have enough time to record all her bullshit. If evil had an address it would be her house number!

What's so funny is that I presented her and my adult son with a copy of, "Daddy Had to Say Goodbye" because it was all based upon my telling him it's not his fault that I had to leave his life. She and he thought it was great right up until the point where she read of how she tried to sabotage my relationship with my son by telling him that, "Daddy would be mean to him when it gets dark outside." Who the fuck does that to a three year old child?

I'm of the understanding that she has debased me, defiled me and I don't know what the fuck else words to use, but yeah she don't dig me. You see, she is that type of person that must destroy me so others won't hear the truth. First of all, she is a badge bunny, okay that was her thing, well I thought that would all change once we were married, think again Chum! I have no chance of having any type of relationship with my son because she has so severely poisoned his mind with what a bad man I was. Yeah okay, my hatred for her could point to the direction of at least a killer. All right, what's next?

Frederic: So your fifth wife's name was Steph and is she still with us?

Me: You know, I don't know. I've just lost track with her and that's fine by me. She again made life choices which caused me to gasp, I guess you could say I have no desire to speak with her. I don't hate her, I just think she's fucking nuts. Hell, she had to have been, she married me didn't she! Everything you read about her is extremely accurate, it's the same as I've written about all of my wives. They are who they were for their own reasons, I had no control over who they were. I did however have control over how I may have affected them and for that I have to take a step back and apologize. What would she say if she were to be interviewed? I honestly don't know, I have no idea. So now if we're through the wife's dark alleyways, there have been a few lovers on the side which don't deserve any level of mention, they were all after something, I was after something, we both got what we wanted at the time, that's all, that's all it was.

  Marge: David the final chapter, chapter #36, "The transition" was incredibly eye-opening! It was like I had no eyelids left at all. You just put everything out there, you spoke of every human's weaknesses while using yourself as the example. You talked about how severely broken you were which was of your own making. You took full responsibility and you told those young people, "Here's how I got out from under it." You identified the problem and you gave the solution. A solution that would work for everyone. David, I think this is your finest book. I've read all eight of your books and they're all wonderful and they all have an extreme power in your message of redemption but your first book, "Daddy Had to Say Goodbye" belongs somewhere of great importance for the entire world to see.

  Me: Yeah honey, yeah I see it. I've had to pay a fortune to develop a website to show it off and of course I dance with it on Facebook but will it ever be a required reading at some point in my life? Never, not at all, far too much truth, too much honesty and of course let's all remember that I have a filthy mouth. No, it's one of those things that may or may not ever be discovered but by only a handful of you. So your question is, why do I write? I write to stay alive, that's where my heart is. Every stroke of an ink pen causes my heart to beat, if I lay down the pen I'm in fear that I would lose my life, my spiritual life, my emotional life. I'm not willing to risk losing any of that, so yeah I think we need to call it a day kids, you all look a bit beat up. I feel beat up and more than just a bit, so I'm going to go home and pet my dogs and have a nice nap. Maybe eat some potato chips and leave crumbs on the couch. Heather loves me for that, I'll see you all tomorrow, I'll be at the front desk at 8:00 a.m.

Chapter 10
The Wake-Up Call

I startled awake, I didn't know where I was for a few moments. I thought I was in a hotel room listening to the phone ringing for a morning wake up call. Well that wake up call came as an epiphany and I was pissed off! I was pissed off at myself for being so ignorant. Yes, I know that these people remind me that I've got to give this group a nice name. I'll have to think on that too but what's got me so pissed off at the moment is that yes, they've been very open about their goals as to running for public office but what they haven't talked about but they're going to, is the fact that once they get seated in office they are going to use me for months, if not years of hearings, to go after the people they promised they would take care of during their candidacy. Their 'War Chest' must be damn deep and wide. Hell, they didn't blink for a nano-second when I told them I wanted twenty grand for Tim's services. Yes, I'm going to be their puppet in their dog and pony show and those fuckers are going to try to drag me through every hearing. I will be their star witness and I will be held on a stand to testify for the rest of my life. I don't trust any of these people, I sure as hell am not going to show or play my 'hole card'! Perhaps I better think about this, I've got to get away and get out from underneath this bullshit. I'm all for their goals but I'm not going to be a part of that. When I'm done, I'll be done! They can wipe their ass with their subpoenas and demands, I'm still a free man, at least I hope I am! If they do come for me, they damn well better get right with Jesus before they ring my doorbell!

    I went into the lobby to meet the Gang for the 8:00 meeting in the lobby but I arrived there at 7:00. I wanted to see who the most dedicated of them all was. I know it's just a brief elevator ride down to the lobby for all of them but I wanted to see who is in it to truly win It. I was not disappointed, there sat that lovely little Abby, wearing blue jeans and a light sweater, that sweater did nothing as well as the blue jeans to hide her shapely, well filled out youthful body. Her hair was all but perfect. I don't even think she was wearing makeup as she has porcelain skin and full eyebrows, nothing painted on for this girl. I found that quite refreshing!
    I had parked in the back of the hotel so I strolled towards the front lobby. A well dressed middle-aged man approached Abby, leaned down and said something that I couldn't hear and then disappeared. Abby came to her feet, quickly turned

and smiled as I approached her. My only thought was, "Jesus Christ, she has a handler too! That guy was tipping her off as to my approaching her. Who the fuck is he and where the hell did he even come from?" I guess I better get on my pony and ride, when it comes to paying attention.

Me: Good morning sweetheart, couldn't sleep?

Abby: David, I slept quite well thank you. I've been waiting for you because I don't want to miss one moment of not being in your presence. There's so much you've already taught me and I know I have so much more to learn. To learn about everything, people, life and places. Although I'm quite independent, I've also been well sheltered. I'm learning how to breathe from you, I'm learning how to slow down and process rather than acting without thought like I'm just another robot of some sort. I want to learn how to free think freely like you do. All I've ever done in my life is plan and rehearse everything I do. I want to learn to trust my gut and my thoughts. I want to learn to trust or even maybe develop instincts that I've truly never had before. Everything has come from either a book or lectures. You have this innate ability to just let it flow. I know that speaks highly of your level of confidence and I would be the last person to accuse you of having arrogance but you're so incredibly confident. You trust yourself, you believe in who you are, in what you do and what you say, which makes you so believable of course. David I'm here to serve you in any fashion I possibly can.

Me: Baby at this moment the best way you can serve me is to allow me to escort you into the restaurant. I trust you haven't been awake long enough to have had breakfast?

As we sat in the restaurant I had a bit of sadness come over me with watching Abby sitting and eating her meal. It was almost like she was in a military school of some kind. She repositioned the silverware and turned her coffee cup handle to the 3 o'clock position the moment we were seated. Everything was squared away, she was mechanical in the way she held her fork, the way she put her food to her fork without scraping her fork on the plate. Yeah she's had some training, maybe finishing school of some kind but yeah, I can see why she wants to break loose of all this bullshit. I looked over at her and I said, "Abs watch this," as I took my fork and banged it into my plate, scooped up my scrambled egg and jammed it in my mouth. "Abs honey, your turn."
Abby first looked at me with a quizzical glance as if I had actually given her permission. She slapped her fork on her plate, scooped up her scrambled eggs and slammed them in her mouth, the same as I had.

Abby giggled and then she started to laugh as she said, "Damn that felt good! I'm going to have to learn how to eat like a person instead of a proper lady!"

Me: I guess that finishing school didn't have much to do with teaching you how to live, they just taught you how to act and you act like you've been taught, if not programmed. There's almost nothing natural in any of your movements. Follow my lead and I will teach you how to breathe. I don't know anything about you being a lady or how to tone you down a bit to where you're actually comfortable but I think you're on the right path. Yes baby it's hard to be you when you don't know who that "you" is, right?

    Abby: David you're singing the song of my people, I've always been controlled and nice but I've never felt comfortable. I was a misfit that fit in with everyone. The only person I didn't fit in with was me. I don't like being rigid but I don't know how to be anything else. I now have hope that you will give me the proper direction?

    Me: Oh, you're going to trust me for directions? Do this sweetheart, give me a big smile, okay now take your finger with your gorgeous polished nails and put it in the crevice of each of your brilliant white teeth as though you're trying to pick something from your teeth, maybe a piece of bacon or something heavy.

    Abby: But David, I don't have anything stuck in my teeth.

    Me: Precisely my love, maybe it's time you learn how to pick your teeth in public just like the rest of the world does. You're not selling your soul to be a part of something larger than you. Once we get down to the nut cutting, I'm sure you'll find that little of what you've been taught has not served you, just others. Yeah baby you were trying to be a marionette. I have to tell you sweetheart that I'm bothered by your fingernails, they are perfectly formed, shaped and obviously been professionally polished. Not everything has to be done to absolute perfection. I think when we take our break today, I'm going to take you down to the beach. There's about a sixteen mile long area along the coastline where the heavy wave action crushes rocks. At the far north end, there are boulders the size of a smart car. A mile away there are smaller boulders, two miles further down the beach the boulders are the size of party type beach ball. Another mile the rocks are the size of a softball, those shrinking rocks then become coarse beach sand. As you walk further south the sand becomes finer and finer from centuries of ice shifting and crushing wave action, all compliments of our maker. I'm going to take you down there and teach you how to skip rocks and then we're going to play in the sand of all different course levels. When everything is said and done, your nails will become just a bit jagged and ragged, the high sheen of your fingernail polish will be worn and in hopes that you'll have a healthier glow about yourself. You've got to step out of that briefcase world you've been living in if you want to learn how to breathe, that's a start. Hell, maybe we will build a sand castle with a three car garage!

Chapter 11
The Attempt

At 7:50 a.m. (10 minutes prior to our meeting at the front desk) Tim phoned me. He said, "I need to see you in the garage in the sealed parking area right away." Of course I immediately started towards the garage but something told me that this could be something different once I was out of visual sight of hotel guests and employees. I drew my weapon while going down that maze of service hallways and softened my steps. I called Tim on his cell phone and said, "Come and open the door for me, I didn't want to step into a large open room with plenty of hiding and ambush sites."

I listened for footsteps as Tim approached the door. I only heard footsteps from one person, he opened the door and smiled. I said, "Fucker, something bad better be happening or I'm going to bust your ass, don't you put me through this super spy bullshit, get over here. We're going outside the other way."

Tim grinned as he said, "It's not that serious, I just wanted a minute with you. Well security contacted me last night, actually quite early this morning. The lawyers demanded that security take them up the elevator and give them full access to the Eagles Nest. Luckily hotel security is very well trained here. They contacted me immediately. I approached the three women and ask them if they would like to go into lockdown, "Ladies you don't have any fucking right of any kind to enter David's private quarters, unless invited."

Me: What do you think they were up to?

Tim: God only knows but I sure am going to ask them, what I need is your permission to send them all packing if I don't like their attitude.

Me: Timmy my lad, I trust you implicitly. If you're looking at some kind of devious bullshit going on, call them out. If we have to, we will send them all the fuck home. I still have a hole-card I can play and walk away from this entire gig. This is about them receiving governorships, it has nothing to do with me. I'm just one of their game board pieces, I don't give a fuck if they become Governors or not. I don't trust half of what they've told me about what they would do as governors. We've both heard the promises and we've all seen the results unless of course you're a fuckin Democrat. All they promise to do is cripple our nation. Yeah they really did follow through on that promise.

Tim: What happened to the simpler days where we just woke up in the morning, scratched our balls and decided whether or not we're going to go fishing or sleep in, what happened to those days? Now everything is so damn heavily scheduled. Heavily controlled with, this must to happen, that has to happen. We have to go here, we have to go there. Where the fuck does all of this madness come from?

Me: I couldn't tell you pal. I haven't signed up for that game, I do as I fucking wish when I want and I do it the way I want or I do nothing.

Let's do this, why don't you hop into the lobby and corral those six wonderful human beings, escort them to the Seafarer Room and invite them to have a seat and have two security officers confiscate their property, all of it and lock them in. And you know what pal, we're going to let them wait! There's a lot of different ways to spank people, I think this is one of the better ones. Fuck them! You and I are going to go for breakfast, hell we might be gone all fuckin morning long, let them wait.

Tim and I went to the security office to review the tapes and to read the officers reports of what this bullshit was all about. Well security was tipped off on the alarm to the floor below mine. It was set off by somebody trying to put keys into the lock to release the elevator to the next floor, my floor! The tape showed several of the six trying to put many different keys into the lock. Two of them each had a bottle of wine in their hands and four of them had a bottle of wine in each hand. The wine bottles were sitting on the shelf in the security office. They looked awfully expensive. I Googled the name of the wines and it had to do with 'Domino's Estate' and 'Dominus USA

Bordeaux' . It was some kind of high-end Napa Valley shit. It showed that it was $349.95. I don't know if that was a per bottle or per case rate, I don't know shit about wine. I don't need to know. The reports read that when those six were challenged they simply said, "Oh we were just going to go upstairs and watch the ships go by and drink our wine." The report went on to say that they were escorted out of the elevator and back to their rooms with a strong admonishment that they were not to leave their rooms for the rest of the evening.

    Tim and I went back to the Seafarer Room two hours later. When I stepped in, there were some angry faces. I started with, "So you people are pissed off that you're in custody, if you will? Yeah what you all did is called attempted burglary, I've got plenty of friends with blue shirts and badges that would be more than happy to give you all a lift to the same destination. Here's the deal children, your entitlement that you've enjoyed throughout your lifetimes stopped when you broke the threshold of the doors of this building.

    This is not your game, this is my game. I own this fucking game, my friends own this fucking game, you own nothing in this facility, nothing other than the clothes you brought in. So you just thought you would party in my home and sit and watch the ships go by and enjoy the moonlight and the stars twinkling? There's only two people I've allowed to ever consume alcohol in my private (and that's right) it's my private residence, where I have so graciously allowed you to enter into to do the work necessary. These aren't your fuckin digs kids!

Now if you're ready to go to work and lose that pompous attitude that you all carry, I'm ready but I'm coming at you hard. I'm pissed off and I'm done with fucking around. Here's something I want you to understand, even before we leave this goddamn room. I know exactly what your game is and I'm somewhat under the impression that you designed this game. This is not about bad people trying to get me, it's you trying to get attention by promoting the bad people to get me. There's even a pretty good chance that you might be the bad people and this whole thing is a setup for you to shine. This is just one big fucking media circus that you people have obviously paid to have produced. That ain't the way it's going to fly kids. I'll do my deal, my way until I'm done with it. Now gather your things for this next session. I believe we're on book #2, "Flesh Of A Fraud/The Lies We Tell ourselves."

Chapter 12
Digging In

    Me: All right you guys let's have it. On to book #2 and again, the story lines are lovely but it's the characters, those are the people that you want to testify, am I not right? Some of these characters I'd like to have to testify for me, if they were all real but many of them are real. Some of them you will have no access to, others, well that's entirely up to them. Doris you're the leader of the pack let's start with you

    Doris: David, with just reading the reader's reviews the first thing that pops into my head is that I'd like to meet these people that wrote those reviews. Are any of these people accessible and are any of these people in fact characters within your books? Is that a fair question?

    Me: Yeah that's a fair question, the reader reviews are 100% legit and without embellishment. They were printed as they were written, word for word. Some of the characters in all of my books are real, some are not, again that's what makes it a novel.

So we're looking at 365 pages of a story. It's an ongoing story because each book is a part of my entire life story.

Doris: Well we all know we're already in Dutch with you for trying to break into your private dwelling and for that, I want to personally apologize, oh and if I may, are we going to get our wine back?

Me: No kids, those bottles of wine have put large smiles on the faces of a couple of desk clerks, bellhops, maids and maintenance workers. It should please you ladies and gentlemen to know that Tim's wife is a rather frugal low end 'box wine' drinker. I think you may have converted her with your fine selections of bottled wines. You must know that those people would never, ever dream of paying that kind of money for wine. So to answer your question, you're not going to get your wine back because it's already been given away. It's gone, I will consider it as your fine for attempted burglary. Unless of course you would like to contact our local police department and try to explain to my friends in blue how you felt you were entitled to commit a burglary? I don't think that will bode well for any of you. I suggest you drop it while I'm still willing to allow you to. And no, you will not be allowed to ever bring alcohol into this room. As I mentioned earlier, only two other people have been allowed to drink in my quarters and they were the two Physicians that saved my life. I gave them this suite for a week for their honeymoon before they went off to parts unknown. I'm done with that shit, on to the book young lady, focus.

Marge: Well David, just in the introduction you gave me the shivers with the quote, "Is this the day, is this the day that I finally decide that the pain of living is far worse than the pain of dying?" Holy Christ David, that didnt just throw me deep into my seat, it fucking slammed me! I was actually reading that book on a flight, the passenger next to me obviously saw me transition and asked if I was okay and if I had a fear of flying and he went on and on and on. I just closed up your book and put it back in my purse. I knew that this is nothing to read in public. David, I agree with your declaration that we're going to stay with the characters. However, in some areas I must beg to differ. I think it's important that people see your human side. Your introduction page perfectly defines everything about Minnesota winters. I loved it when you write about going outside for a smoke as your nose hair shattered and fell to your feet, how you lose weight from shoveling snow and how your jacket sleeves and gloves glisten from wiping snot from your constantly running nose with snow piled up to a giraffe's ass! That's the pure poetry of Minnesota winters. I spent a winter here when I was a kid, not as far north as you are but in the central part of the state. I enjoyed the way you talked about having a few pals from what you call, "Drunks R Us". That was hilarious. If I may finish my argument, I read about your cousin Rolene and the closeness you two shared and yet lived a great distance apart. Yes I agree David, love is love. David that, that thing with you and Heather sitting on your deck listening to the police scanner and suddenly you hear the location and the description of an electric mobility cart on top of a woman lying in the roadway and you knew, you actually knew at that very moment that that was your cousin Rolene. You further knew that she was dead. David those things have to come out, they're going to try to paint you as a monster and a killer. They want the world to see you as a ruthless mass murderer!

Me: Marge, put that away for a while, I'll consider it, now let's move on. Doris, you're next what's up with you?

Doris: Well again David, these characters at the bookstore, real or not?

Me: They are very much alive, well and real and yes, they are my friends.

Doris: The way you stepped in and took charge of that whole book signing thing was brilliant. You brought people together who had no hope. Several of those people and not just the bookstore people were ready to accept their fate. The young lady from the hotel here was about to lose her job, the newspaper reporter who again was about to lose her job and of course the owner of the hotel chain was about to take his own life. You mustered those people and you brought them to a height that none of them had ever known before. You taught them how to succeed and what I gleaned from all this, said that these were all people who stopped dreaming. Their fears stepped in front of their dreams and they were held hostage within themselves. You rescued these hostages, you gave them hope, they found a renewed purpose and they all found success! David, that is a beautiful story.

    Phil: David I can't tell you what my favorite page or chapter is, I just love your writing, I love your books, I love your heart that goes into your writing. I was really taken back in the first page of chapter #3 where the character Missy asked if she could bring her parents to meet you and I think I can quote this, "No you cannot, you take me to meet your parents, they outrank me and you should know that!" That was beautiful, the respect you showed towards her and her parents and the lesson that you laid at her feet in just a couple brief words was a spiritual moment for me. If I may, I would now like to ask you if the Quinn's are real people.

    Me: Okay guys here is where it starts to get sticky. Are the Quinn's real people? Would you like them to be real people? I know why you're asking of course, we would all like to have friends like the Quinn's, once you get past their up-tight bluster, they're wonderful human beings, probably much like your own selfs. Sadly we're still stuck in the Bluster and Bullshit phase of our relationship here today. In addressing your question as to the realness of the Quinn's, it's time for a bit of caution and this shit ain't nothing to play with. Children, there are people in this world, good people, good people who are forced to do bad things to bad people. The Quinn's are two of those people, yes they're good people without question because they do bad things to bad people. That's your true question isn't it? The Quinn's are who they appear to be. When they want to be seen in that particular type of light. So here's where the cautionary tale must develop, don't fuck with me or the Quinn's!

Let me tell you guys this, there are several characters throughout my books that are all but apparitions, it's like if you were out on Lake Superior today. There's always an early morning mist and fog. You will be trolling in a small boat trout fishing in the fog and suddenly out of that fog looms a monstrous ship bearing down on top of you and you only have seconds to steer away from that ship to avoid their drafting waves that will capsize you. Your life jackets won't save you, you will die from exposure in the freezing waters of Lake Superior in just a few minutes, no matter what time of year it is. I hope that defines those characters I'm telling you about. Now, the people I've written about are real when it's time to be, but they disappear like the apparition in the clouds or the fog or in a mind that has had too much wine. Okay what else?

Frederic: I liked it when Seth actually dressed you down a bit. I don't think it was a false humility that you were trying to display. I think that's how you are but when you defined yourself to him as a, 'tag along nobody author' he took great exception to that. Is there actually a Walker's bookstore?

Me: No Freddy, the Walker book name is a developed name, but is there a bookstore in Duluth that I have my books in, yes of course. The Wakers are real people and dear friends of course.

Frederic: David I loved it, I absolutely loved the way you drew people in for your first book signing when you played that hands in the air game to ask how many people have considered writing a book. Again you extend your hand of validation to so many people in so many different ways that everyone that walks away from you feels that blessing. The way that you pulled Seth and Mary from the brink of financial disaster and without any realization of you being recognized or being paid for it, again that speaks of the caliber of your character and I think we need to highlight your character because that's something that you can't fake, nobody can. So yeah I think a number of these people have to be brought forward as character witnesses. By now they may have already been spoken to by the enemy camp.

Me: No chance of that Freddy boy, they would never speak out of school, if you will. These people are my friends. Firstly if they were approached they would have their own questions as to the validity of the questioners. These are not stupid people, they get it, they get the big picture, secondly they would immediately excuse themselves at that moment and phone me. No, they have never been sworn to secrecy, at least by me. If you're asking if they would lie for me, fucks yes they would all lie for me, are you shitting me? We are Pals, maybe you need to watch the movie, 'Young Guns' when Emilio Estevez (as Billy The Kid) speaks of the definition of Pals. Of course I'm not foolish enough to think that you would lower yourselves to watch what I would refer to as, a modern day classic Western. I will give you that definition; "Friends are people that you might fight for. Pals are people that you would kill for." Here is a FYI for you all whether you want to know it or not. "Billy The Kid" was murdered by his trusted and long time friend Sheriff Pat Garrett On July 14th 1881. The following day Billy was buried in Fort Summer's old military cemetery. Henry McCardy. a.k.a William H. Bonney, a.k.a. Billy The Kid, was laid next to two of his outlaw friends, there was only one carved headstone for the three which read, "PALS." And no, don't even ask me if I ever killed for a Pal.

    Phil: That whole thing about you taking Vicki up to that hotel roof-top restaurant that revolves around the city and your forethought to both bring her flowers to share with some of the restaurant staff and how you presented her with two, one-of-a-kind custom-made pieces of jewelry from your other friend but I don't think I can trust that. I don't think that came from that gentleman, Paul Roberts. I think that bracelet and necklace came from you, true or false?
    Me: Here's my best answer, shut the fuck up! Now let's move on.
    Phil: When you gave the description of validation about it being a rare gift that very few receive and how we don't look at each other anymore. How we just have mechanical 'thank yous' and 'have a nice day' greetings and we're off to the next big deal. I get and agree with your entire statement of how our society is so fucking self-absorbed and so

shallow that it's sickens me too, when I read about my own weaknesses.

    Me: Let me say this to you Phil and the rest of you folks, you're spending too much time stroking me. I don't need it, part of what you're saying, yes I appreciate hearing but I also know that you're trying to get on my good side before I bounce your asses out to the curb. Word has it that you three principal ladies spend a great deal of time in the gym every night, as well as the six of you swimming lap after lap after lap in the pool. Well that's cute and all, physical wellness is important of course but here's where you're missing out. What have you done for your spiritual, emotional and psychological wellness? I dare say, very little. You are taken back by my simpleness and I do believe that you would like to be a bit more like me. Well here it is kids, lifting weights, swimming laps and that cutesy bicycle bullshit, yes does improve and maintain muscular structure but that muscular structure does not come at the time you're tearing down muscle. It comes during the rest period when your amino acids kick in. That's where the muscle or the tone is developed, not the exercise itself. In that same vein, if you were to exercise kindness, understanding, compassion and a litany of other swell words that describe what a good person is, you all would be far ahead of the game. Exercise your kindness, your goodness and you will learn what your purpose in life truly is. Slamming weights around and pounding law books is not a purpose, gaining wealth and political power is not a purpose. Purpose comes

THE GHOST IN OUR LOCKERS

from within, not what you do but who you are. Identify who you are today and then identify who you would like to be tomorrow and for all the days to follow. If you want respect, become respectful. That's it for today's lecture series. I'm done with you guys, I need a nap, now get out of here.

Chapter 13
Calling in a Debt

I woke from my nap with laughter. I had this crazy dream that I had decided to run for mayor of Duluth and switch things up while I bring the city back to the people and not the politicians. The corruption runs deep here and it runs all throughout the state. Our empty minded mayor is well entrenched with the number of schemers in other political offices. All of Minnesota politics is filthy with slimeball people that give you nothing and take everything, nobody is in politics at least in this state, to "Serve the People." It's strictly about serving themselves and it sickens me. I would like to make that difference but I'm too old and too tired, but it sure would be fun.

Shortly after dressing and brushing my teeth my phone rang and it was Tim. He wanted to meet with me, he told me that all of the information came through, he thought we'd better sit down with it.

Tim: Well David, our initial research on who the fabulous three are, fell a bit short but you'll find this interesting. The three, what is it you call them, understudies? These understudies are actually more interesting than your principal attorneys for my nickel, the most interesting has to be Frederic. Dig this, Freddy boy was defending a fellow in a simple divorce case which exploded into multiple felonies for the male. The petitioner was the female and the petitioner's family were quite well to do. It was quite obvious to everyone that those felony charges were manufactured by the wife's family, the extremely well to do family I may add. Well it was again quite obvious that the judge was deeply embedded in the families pockets. Frederic did all he could on behalf of his client but every maneuver he attempted, the judge shut down. Frederic got more than a bit pissed off and told the judge in open court that he felt the judge had received a bribe. The judge sent him to three days in the county jail and during those three days the judge was very much proactive in attempting to have Frederic censored and disbarred. This squabbling went on between Frederic and a judge for a couple months and when all the dust had finally settled the judge was removed from the bench and was disbarred and cannot practice law anywhere in this nation! So you want to know where the power sits in your room, it sits clearly in Frederic's lap. That lad is your Powerhouse, when you go over the financials you'll see that everyone is well healed if you look at their campaign contribution funds (although they haven't even announced yet) you'll see that they've got some power support and a lot of money that's why they didn't balk when you told them to lay down twenty grand for me. They've got lots of twenty grands to throw around. Ole Freddy boy is pretty much a self-made guy and he's also pretty much middle class across the board. No pompous bullshit he's pretty much, what you see is what you get. Who does that remind you of David?

    Me: Fuck you buddy, I'm for sale, it's just that nobody cares to buy me! Ain't that a bitch? Let's understand that we still need one other team player that I want to bring in, yes we're going to absorb Freddy. We're going to bring him into our camp. I don't even know what his future hopes and plans are but we're going to find out. Here's something I need to tell you about sweet, adorable Phyllis and Abby. They are the only true alleys of this group of six. When it comes to Abby, I believe that I can trust her more than any of the others combined, so as it stands now the score is 4 to 5. You, me, Phyllis and Freddy boy, against the others but I'm about to bring another person on board it has to do with a friend of Phyllis's, oh and just so you know, Phyllis has her sights on me and you know if I were a single man, yeah she would be shooting bull's eyes for sure but we can't let that happen. I cannot meet and I will not meet with any one of these women on a one-to-one and of course the question is, who is it I mistrust, them or me? I would have to say at this point that it's probably split down the center. So I'm going to bring Phyllis in and the three of us are going to have a conversation and that's when I'll tell you and her about bringing in another party.

I rang up Phil's cell phone and she answered, I said, "Security will be down to your room if that's where you are right now, security will escort you up to the Eagles Nest. Tim is here and we want to speak with you, be ready in 5 minutes.

Tim: Are you going to call me in on this? Please don't make me have to question my trust level with you. What the fuck are you going to do with Abby, it seems as though there's a young lady who is absolutely enthralled with you.

Me: I've used my good looks, wit and charm all my life to get laid. Now I'm going to use those same traits to get free of all this crap. There's a young lady who will be my second Ace in the Hole.

Tim and I were both standing at the elevator door when it opened with Phil and her security escorts. Phil had a look of dread on her face as though she was in some kind of trouble. I gave her a hug and said, "Baby everything's all right, as a matter of fact you're about to receive a promotion, come with me."

I brought her into the Eagles Nest and sat her down and said, "Give me the cell phone number for your buddy Amy." Phil had a strange look about her that I couldn't quite read. I was wondering if maybe she was feeling a little jealous that I wanted to talk to Amy.

I called Amy on my cell phone so she could see the caller ID. She answered as I said, "Amy you know who this is by my caller ID, give my friend Tim your particulars. We're going to dial you up for a video chat. Amy and Tim talked for a few minutes and I said, "Okay honey, hang up and we'll ring you back in just a moment, I want you to be in a secured area, I want this conversation only between us guys, fair enough?

> Amy: Yes sir absolutely, I'll go into my office.
> Me: That's great babe, talk to you in a minute.

I had Tim throw the phone call to the large screen so Amy could see the three of us at the same time together as well as I wanted to look at her and her surroundings. It has been my experience that a person's office can tell you an awful lot about that person. Just before we went live for our conference call I slid Tim a note asking for Amy's financials, he had it up and on my monitor in just seconds. She was doing quite well for herself, she is a full partner in what seemed to be eight a person Mental Health Service operation.

Me: Well Amy, here I am. What would you like to say to me sweetheart?

Amy: David I I'm just flabbergasted with this call, why would you want to speak with me?

Me: Well sweetheart, your dear friend Phyllis over here spilled the beans. I understand you have the hots for me, is that true?"

We could see Amy blushing and almost giggling. I couldn't tell if she was going to burst out in tears or burst out in laughter. Tim tapped his fingernail on the desktop and mouth the words, "You're a prick." Of course the two girls caught that and we all had brief giggles. I said, "Amy I know little if anything at all about you, only what Phyllis has told me and her name is Phil in this office just so you know. How much do you know about what's going on?"

Amy: Well sir, I know that it sounds strange to hear you call her Phil. Phil and I talk every day. All I know is that you're in some kind of trouble, but she's not really speaking of any confidential conversations, nor have I asked. It's just something none of us do in this business.

Me: Well that's wonderful, I don't believe you, I think you're full of shit actually but okay. I understand that there's eight people in your organization, is that correct and you're all certified headshrinkers right?"

Amy: If you have to call us that, go ahead.

Me: Great, can you break away? Could I hire you for let's say a month? You will come to Duluth and help me with this case, all your expenses will be paid along with your billable hourly rates and your salary. You'll stay here at the Corker Hotel with the rest of the crew and you and Phil can enjoy a pajama party, every night for the entire month! The crew you'll get to meet later on.

Amy: How soon do you need me?

Me: What would you like for breakfast sweetheart?

Amy: My God that soon!
Me: Yeah honey that soon.

Amy sat back in her chair for a moment and went through a couple of what looked to be client schedule books, as she said, "I like my eggs poached, I'll see you in the morning"
Me: Amy girl, you and I are going to get along just fine. I'll pick you up at the airport. Send me a text with your flight information. Do you need a credit card number?
Amy laughed and said, "No we can square that up later, I'm not too concerned about that. I can't wait to finally meet you!" Same on this end sweetie, I'll see you in the morning.

I completely enjoyed Phil's look of bewilderment. I smiled at her and said, "Well go ahead ask.

Phil: I'm not sure if this is any of my business, I'm not sure if I want it to be any of my business?
Me: What's the matter Phil, don't want the competition. Here's the deal sweetheart. Amy is a shrink right and I need someone to examine me and more importantly, I need someone to examine you guys as to who I can trust, what team you all are actually playing for. If this thing's going to have some kind of a jury, I want her to get a read on each jury member. Tim will pull up all the backgrounds on each jury member. We're not going to be blindsided, we're

going to come in with guns drawn. You may see this as my separating you from your other two cohorts and maybe I am. There's a reason for that sweetheart, I trust you. From everything you've told me about Amy you trust her, she trusts you, which makes it simply, quite simply for me to trust her. Once again I'm fighting for my freedom, you people are fighting for positions, there's a hell of a difference between those two. And with that in mind, where does the thrust come from in your group? I know you all have money, I know you all have received campaign contributions that are neatly tucked away for the future. None of you have made any kind of announcement but you can't pull off this kind of campaign with those types of contributions. Who's pushing this wagon? You all have a benefactor for the three of you. I need to know who that is.

    Phil: David as much as I'd like to, there's no possible way I can identify who you like to refer to as our 'benefactor.' Even though you're fighting for your life (I'll do my damnedest to make sure that you walk free and clear) I cannot violate the confidence that was placed in me. Remember this party sponsored us to keep you free, I don't know what your relationship is with this person or persons. I don't even know if you've ever met them or him or her. All I know is that this is as far as I'm going to go with this question. I love you to pieces David, but I won't betray my oath of confidence. I'm sure you can respect that, I hope you can respect me.

    Me: Like I have options?

Tim: So we're bringing in another player to the team? What are you going to do with Frederic?

Me: Frederic is my man! I like ballsy people. Not only that, but he's the humblest of the entire group. He doesn't play dick head games, he just shoots straight from the hip, he kind of reminds me of me, or maybe the me I wish I were, but for now kids, it's not about fighting fair it's about fighting dirty, it sounds like it's going to be that whole David and Goliath bullshit all over again. I gotta find a bigger rock!

So Phil, let me ask you. How do you do with children, do you like them, better yet, do they like you?

Phil: I love children, I can't get enough of my nieces and nephews. I so much wish I had my own children. I guess that'll come at a later time.

Me: So you're not going to shop for a husband, you're going to shop for a father for your unborn children? That's a nice take on things, I wish you well with that plan but in the meantime I want you to have some more training. Poor Tim here, has not left my side or this building for the last several days, he and his wife need a break. I'm sending them to Las Vegas for few or three days, however the fuck that works. I don't know but you get to play nanny.

Phil: What about Amy?

Me: Honey, Amy and I will do just fine. I'll bring you in when the time is right but make no mistake, Amy may be your pal but she is coming to see me and no one else. That's the way it has to be sweetheart, so are you down for doing some babysitting?

Phil: You lousy bastard of course I am. You have such a prick-head way about you, I like that term, 'prick-head' by the way, I think I'll use that quite often throughout our time together, prick-head!

Me: Phil one more thing, think back to when my friends showed up to honor our client attorney privilege contracts. Do you remember that, do you remember who those people were? Yes that's right, there was an active federal judge, an active county prosecutor who is no one to fuck with and the heavily experienced police investigator. Do you recall the admonishment from that federal judge?

Phil: Yeah, yeah we wondered about that. I guess the message is, "Fuck around and find out?" That phrase seems to be going around a lot these days, especially with you but we thought that was quite strange. None of us had ever had a federal judge witness a contract like that.

Me: Oh honey, please don't tell me that I tipped over the Apple Cart? My point sweetheart, is that those were all individual contracts with you as individuals not as a group, but as individuals right? So here's where it gets a little sticky for you, we'll see how well you can play this game. You are bound by contract to not discuss anything between myself and yourself even with your fellow attorneys. *Capiche.*

I don't want Doris or Marge to know about Amy coming and the time I spend with Amy. I may or may not include her with the group. She is coming here as my personal emissary, oh and just so you know, there's another contract that will be Inked and have to do with provider/patient confidentiality. I don't think that's a boundary you or your two Compadres would ever want to try to step across. Remember I have a buddy who likes to trout fish, who likes to shoot my guns and who just so happens to be a federal judge.

    Phil: David you definitely missed your calling, you pull these strategies out of thin air and make them work every time, without even implementing them. You are the epitome of what a devious dick-head is, aren't you?

    Me: Lover child, only when the time calls for it, most often I'm just a smooth furred tiny little kitty cat. Now get the fuck out of here, I got shit to do. Oh honey before you leave, go ahead and make reservations for Tim and his wife, where do you want to stay buddy?

    Tim: Anywhere in Las Vegas where you can't find me, how's that and oh we would like four nights and five days.

    Me: You heard the man Phil, get to it honey, I'm going to go make some popcorn.

Chapter 14
Game On!

What I've always found to be a strange situation is when I and many others ask someone that you trust for their input, as you listen and process what they're saying you somehow at least I do, feel that I'm being moved away from my initial thoughts and my instincts. Sometimes when I am given great counsel, I become resentful. Maybe it's my own ego of thinking, "I should have known this myself!" Maybe I take it as a personal affront when it shouldn't be. When people try to help me I develop this weird kind of frustration, 'anger thinking' that I didn't think of it that, maybe I'm not smart enough to think of that, so I often times ask for advice, but I don't want to use that advise because I feel resentful towards the person that I asked for the advice, how fucked up is that? Yeah, maybe I need to spend some quality time with Amy so we can clear up my fucked headedness. So now I'm still at an impasse with Frederic, do I bring them all in, sit them down on a one to one? Obviously

he's quite bright and what he might lack in tact, he makes up for in intelligence. Whatever he may be lacking he surely does make up in ballsiness. I knew there was something about that guy that was special but holy shit, going after a seated judge, standing in a judge's courtroom and arguing with him?
that prick-head judge sent him to jail for three days, that's the guy I want in my camp, now there's a fucking fighter, I love fighters! I don't think I want to wait to get Amy's take on Freddy. Tim has his own set of skills and I trust him.

    I called Tim and I said, I need a walk buddy. He said he'd be right there. We walked around the hotel a couple times, slipped into a coffee shop and had one of those fancy coffee shop donuts, what are they called? I don't even know what the hell they're called, scones maybe, hell I don't know.

    Me: Tim, how's the wife doing with your trip to Vegas? Tim smiled as he said, "You have to buy her a new outfit you prick-head! I like that prick-head stuff, when I think of you. I'm going to use it often. She's pretty excited but she's a little apprehensive about Phil looking after our children, but they're going to meet this evening we're going to have dinner with her.

    Me: Oh cool, so let me ask you, is that why you think I called you up here, dick- head?

    Tim: You son of a bitch, I never assume anything when it comes to you, other than you're going to throw me a curve ball or a sinker, a slider or whatever the fuck you got in your six finger ball glove. Go ahead and light me up, old wise one.

Me: Well I want to bring Fred over to our side. You've already checked him out, what do you think?

Tim: Dave I think you're smart not to trust this crew as a whole, there's always somebody that's going to be influenced by an outside source. There's always somebody that a promise was made to. These broads all have plenty of money but they don't have the power money, money doesn't always buy power, favors buys power so yeah they're all susceptible and I think you're smart to get your guns in order. Amy looks pretty solid on paper. I think I want to interview Phyllis first as to her take on Amy.

Me: You might be right but I think there's someone else you might want to interview and that's me about Phyllis. Buddy boy, I came way too damn close to jumping on her bones, which tells me I can't trust myself as I once could. So I'll need a buffer out of the security team for the hotel here. Who would you suggest to play your role while you're gone spending your kids college funds and grandkids inheritance?

Tim: David every one of these people on staff are rock solid as you well know. You're asking who would be as trustworthy as I am? I'd like you to know there's not another soul on this planet that is as trustworthy as I am, as intelligent and charming as I am, fuck you pick, any one of them, you dick-head! For my nickel it would be Pete, he's the same type of sarcastic prick that you are. I think you'd enjoy his humor and he, like all the rest, is a total badass. You want me to ring him up?

Me: Yeah let's do that, have him come up here and we will indoctrinate him.

Pete was the right choice of course. I don't think he ever stopped grinning, he had this look about him like, "I'm the most comfortable mutherfucker in the entire northern hemesphere." Yeah Pete and I will do just fine together. Shortly after we briefed Pete I received the call that I was expecting and it came pretty hard.
Doris: David we need to talk. I don't like what you're doing, you can't be doing this to us. You're trying to drive a wedge between us. We can't have that, we have to be one cohesive unit, that's your only chance!
Me: Cute, in truth, it's your only chance! You dolls have been doing some end runs on me and I don't fucking like it!
Doris: David we're developing a strategy, we're trying to keep you out of the loop so you can get the rest you need. Let us do what we do and don't worry about what's going on. At some point you've got to put your trust in us 100%!
Me: Well yeah you're right babe, how about the eight of us meet in the private dining room in the restaurant. Yeah you're right honey, we need to clear the air, let's meet in another hour, that will be at 4:00.

As I was about to hang up with Doris, she still had a hard edge in her voice. I guess she was pissed off. Yeah I get it but they're not fighting for me, they're fighting for them and that's what has to remain in the forefront of my mind. I'm still a party of one when it comes down to it all.

I still needed to bring Freddy up for a private conversation. Tim went down and got him and brought him up.

Me: Fred where'd you come from, how'd you get pulled into this group?

Frederic: Well I guess it was kind of a fluke. I'm not quite ready yet to call it a blessing but I first met Doris during a thunderstorm four years ago. I was leaving the University Library which is kind of down in a bit of a bowl if you will. It was dark and we had one hell of a rainstorm, the parking lot was flooding. She had a flat tire and a very nice car. I think it was like a super Lexus or something I don't know but it was a high end custom without question. I thought she needed help so I had her open her trunk and I jacked up her car and changed her flat tire so she could drive out of the water. Well that's the first time we met, she thanked me and I went on my way and thought nothing more of it, but when I had a bit of a verbal scuffle with the judge that put me in jail for three days and I fought back and had him disbarred, Doris reached out to me and offered me a job. I already had a job with another firm that was paying quite handsomely. Doris doubled that, so yeah I've been working with Doris's firm for almost three years now. When all of this is said and done I will be a full partner. That is if we don't fuck it up.

Me: As in if we don't fuck it up as in, David goes to prison kind of fuck up is that what you're talking about?

Frederic: David I don't believe that anyone here is going to allow that to happen. I know you don't trust any of us and I understand that but what are your other options? You can't shoot the entire fucking state of Minnesota!

Me: You got a point there, old son. Yeah you've got a point but somehow I find myself asking, "Would I trust my bank card to a street junkie so he could buy a sandwich? It's kind of the same thing, different venue of course but I'm still feeling greatly at risk, maybe I need to get a second or third passport. Maybe I need to do that old Mafia style shit where they dip their finger tips in acid to remove their fingerprints. God damn, if that wouldnt be painful enough maybe then throw in a little bit of facial reconstruction surgery and whatever the fuck else I need to do. None of that sounds too exciting, yeah I'm fucked aren't I? So we're down to it's you or it's no one.

Everyone was in their place in the private dining room when I walked in at 10 minutes past 4:00. I love people who are punctual. It's all about respect. Some say if you're late it's because you're telling others that you've got bigger fish to fry. As far as I'm concerned I'm the only fish in this entire fucking pond.

Me: Let's see the hands of those that are pissed off at me to no end right now.

Of course they're all too smart for any of them to raise their hand but you could feel the heavy vibe in the room.

Me: Guys I have a lengthy history of being fucked over by attorneys. Suddenly now I should lay my life before your feet and have you do as you may with me? You really think I'm going to let that fly? I will trust you as far as I can but you have to know that the nice federal judge person wasn't bullshiting, not one fuckin iota. I do have to tell you that it is quite enjoyable to be the favorite son of someone with such immense power.

Marge: Yeah David that's lovely, but you need to remember that we all know where you've been, where do you think we came from? We came from your people, your big, big people sent us. When do we get to get back to your books and your writings that have set the world on fire. We really do have to focus on that, we don't know what the timeline is from the enemy camp. They could call us to Chambers in the next hour if they want to, we have to get on and stay on task.

Me: Swell, yeah I agree. I'm bringing in one more person, you'll meet her tomorrow morning. Her name is Amy. Phil can fill you in about Amy. Amy is here as my personal assistant, she's a psychologist, she will be here to look over me or look after me or whatever she's going to do. I'm sure she could work up some kind of reports for you guys for my defense but more importantly she's here to observe me in my daily wellness or lack thereof. I've yet to meet Amy but I trust her implicitly. If she feels that these activities are harming me she'll pull the plug and I'll let her do it. My only true loyalty belongs with my wife Heather. That's who Amy will be answering to if you will, not to any of you, not to me, just to Heather and of course there is a patient/doctor confidentiality agreement.

    So for right now, we will do nothing with the case until Amy is seated beside me. Tim will be stepping out for a few days, his replacement's name is Pete and Pete's got the goods so you don't want to push him. He too is my personal emissary until Tim returns in a few days. I'm sure you'll treat Pete with a very same level of respect as you have Tim, but for now children there's a van outside waiting for us and the Shrine Circus is in town. Yep we're going to hit up the Shrine Circus, cotton candy, peanuts, popcorn and all the other goodies that come along with it. That's right boys and girls, we're going to see the circus.

Chapter 15
The Ringer

I was waiting at the gate exit when Amy's plane landed. It's interesting that it's called an International Airport which it is, but there is only one entry and one exit to the one jetway. There are no shops and no concourse. There are no amenities of any kind until you go past security then it's just a small grill restaurant and bar. When you're seeing off or waiting for a passenger there's no place to sit. You just stand by one of two of the carousels and you wait. Well of course, I looked up Amy through Facebook and Google. If her photos were not enhanced with those ridiculous filters, she is an extremely attractive young woman. Not unlike the others, who are all total babes, these women look more like they came from a talent agency rather than a prestigious law school. I'm thinking that if there's men sitting at that prosecution table, they're not going to be able to concentrate on anything with these mega babes sitting all around me.

Yeah they've lost the case before they even get started.

It is now 06:55 and here comes Amy. My God she's beautiful, she looks like she just strolled out of makeup from Central Casting. Absolutely a mega babe to be sure! She held herself quite well until about the last 20 feet and suddenly her entire persona changed, her runway model walk with one foot in front of the other style while swaying her hips suddenly vanished. She broke into a run! She was not lady-like at all as she threw herself at me. Of course I hugged her back and suddenly that pretty, smiling beautiful tanned face with high cheekbones had mascara running down it. She was crying quite heavily, sobbing actually as she said, "I never dreamed in my entire life that I'd actually get to meet you. I've studied you for years, I've looked at every picture you've ever had on Facebook and I did that on a regular basis. I don't mind telling you that I have a few of your photographs in frames in my private office at home. You're such a wonderful inspiration to me, it's like I was looking at my dream man. Your pictures would always give me the shivers, good shivers. You are extremely photogenic, I could see your powers and feel your heart in those pictures."

Me: Oh, well that's good. What do you say we go for a spin babe?

I dared not to trade compliments with her, I couldn't trust my trouser brain. I walked Amy to the truck after we picked up her bags at carousel number one. I opened the truck door and placed her bags in the bed of my truck, as it's only a single cab pick-up. As we started to drive from the airport she took off her seatbelt, turned to face me in her seat and reached over and took my hand. She asked, "Is it okay if I do this?"

    Me: Sure babe, as soon as you face forward and buckle your seatbelt.

As we left the airport, I headed northeast.

    Amy: Can I ask you where you're going, where are you taking me? I smiled as I said, "Why do you ask?"

    Amy: I am a licensed pilot. I watched my plane flying from the moment that we were pushed back to taxi and take-off on my wrist watch. I can track a mole tunneling underground from this bad boy. We are traveling in the opposite direction from the city. We should be traveling due south. You are driving northeast, why?

    Me: Be patient sweetheart, we're going to the woods and no, I'm not a killer and yes, you will be able to leave the woods without any harm and under your own power. I want to show you something.

I drove to the area that I described to the lawyers just last night, where I had taken my first wife many years ago during a chance meeting ten years after our divorce. It is where we saw the mama deer and her fawn. I parked the truck on the side of the dirt road. I told Amy to slide out from the driver's side because there is mud in the ditch. She slid out from behind the wheel and I closed the truck door. Amy looked at her bags in the bed of the truck with a questioning look.

Me: Unless you've got gold in those bags I wouldn't worry too much. Nobody comes around here and we don't have the big city assholes like you people have. People leave other people's shit alone, it's a silly little thing called respect.

I walked her down the old, well traveled deer trail and out into the meadow with her wearing several hundred dollars of high heeled shoes.
Me: Does any of this area look familiar to you?
Amy: How can it? I've never been here before, I've never been to Minnesota before.
Me: I'm not talking about that, I'm talking about if someone may have described these surroundings to you.
Amy: Well it sounds just like when you told the ladies about you and your ex-wife Paula and the Doe and Fawn story.

I inwardly smiled because it told me everything I needed to know.

Me: Okay let's get out of here and go get you some breakfast, eggs poached right?

Of course I felt the need to humble her a bit so I took her to my favorite blue collar restaurant on top of Piedmont Avenue, where they give you lumberjack portions that you'll never get anywhere else and for a very fair price, it's a working class place with nothing fancy here. I don't ever remember seeing a coat and tie in this place.

During breakfast I was doing my damnedest not to plot my attack on those people when we got back to the hotel. I was as pissed off as I think I've ever been, they broke the code, they broke the contract! Maybe a federal judge friend of mine needs to help them sharpen their knowledge of, 'Client/Attorney privilege' while warming a steel bench in a fucking jail cell!

As we were finishing breakfast Amy brought out her Platinum (no limit of course) credit card and slid it over to me as though I was to give it to the waitress like it's my card and I'm paying for the meal. I thought that to be quite interesting, the waitress has been a friend of mine for ten years now, so when she came by to give us the check I handed her the 'super card' and said, "Hun pull $50 out of that for your tip, thank you sweetheart." Amy just smiled as she said, "Why the hell not!"

As we got in the truck, Amy asked if it would be okay if we just sat and talked for a moment before we went to the hotel.

Me: Better yet honey, I'll take you to my favorite overlook and you can enjoy the view of the bay of Lake Superior, while we have whatever talk you would like to have.

Amy: David, when I look at you I feel dirty, my thoughts run to crazy extremes that I've never even known before. I've never known of a man like you, I've never looked at a man like you, and when I look into your eyes, I know everything that you've ever written is true. How do I come to terms with my infatuation if not my deepest of love for you? You're kind, you're witty as hell and you're even smarter than you are witty! How do I not get distracted from all that? I'm sure that Elvis must have spent his whole lifetime wishing he looked like you. Hell David, I don't even know why I'm here, you never said, you told me to come and here I am but I don't know why, why am I here? What can I do for you?

Me: Babe you're going to be one of my aces in the hole, you're the only one and listen to me when I say this, you are the only one, do you get that "only" part? That's right, you are the only one that will get to look at my official medical records. Not the ones that everyone else has accessed but the actual ones. You see sweetheart, I've got pals all around and my pals look after me. There are two sets of medical records on file. One sealed, one open only with a request signed only by me and in front of my doctor. Here's the why of your presence, I need you to observe me and report accurately, no fluff, no dramatics, accuracy only! I'm not sure if I want to bring that into a court of law but I may have to as part of my defense. Just as and perhaps even more importantly, I want you to examine Heather. Secondly I want you to tell Heather of your findings as to my health. Understand? Once more, no one is to know of our conversations, absolutely no one! *Capiche?*

Amy: I got it David, you have my word, as a loving friend and as a licensed professional. I will hold the strictest of confidence with all of our conversations and my reports. Can I just say one thing?

Me: Sure honey if that's what you need to do go ahead.

Amy: David, before you pulled over where we parked on that gravel road, I was hoping you would have pulled over a couple of miles back and taken me right in the ditch, next to your truck.

Me: Baby if I wasn't a married-up fella, I would have taken you into that ditch and I would have been on top of you like a black bear on a beehive, but that's not where we are today. I had a conversation just the other day with a friend about fantasies and yes they may give us some level of relief from stress and the reality of everyday life but fantasies do not pay anyone's bills. Now if you are done, let's go meet your pals.

Amy: David, the only friend I have here is Phyllis. I don't know any of these other people, I've never met them.

Me: I think it'll be great when you do, those girls love to strut their stuff and they've definitely got the goods but when they see you, they'll realize that you've got even gooder goods, that should be fun.

Maybe we could have a cat fight in the middle of the lobby!

    Amy: Can I ask one more question, are you going to search me for wires like you did Phil? I felt your gun in your shoulder holster at the airport when I first hugged you, it startled me but god damn it, that turned me on! Just to feel that next to your body and mine made me feel so safe!

    Me: Search you? No chance of that sweet cheeks, remember that you're under contract and your license could be at risk.

Chapter 16
Round #1

My friend Pete and Tim's temporary replacement, (while Tim was off partying his guts out in Las Vegas), was sitting in a vintage high back chair in the lobby. He came to his feet the moment he saw me. I Smiled as I said, "Pete I'd like you to meet my new best friend Amy. Amy girl, this is the man who you don't want to cross. Pete if you wouldn't mind, would you go up and collect Phil and bring her to the Eagles Nest? And Amy, no more of that Phyliss stuff, we call her Phil, got it?"

Pete nodded his head, and said, "Right away sir" as I stepped into the elevator with Amy. It was time for one more test.

As the elevator stopped at the last numbered floor I put my key into the service lock to bring us up to my floor. Amy said, "Oh that's right, I heard about this special lockout system you have, that's pretty cool." I tried to keep a straight face as I realized that I had just been dealt another Ace in the hole! With my luck I'll draw four aces and someone else will draw into a king high straight flush and knock the shit right out of me. I gestured toward the couch and said sweetheart, have a seat I'll be with you in just a moment. I went into my office, closed the door and peeled off my wire and downloaded the conversation's that I had with Amy from the moment I met her at the airport onto a disc and put it in my safe. If all these 'super snooper people' have taught me anything, it is that you trust no one! I couldn't load this into my computers or the cloud or into any handheld device.

    These guys think I have a problem with trust or suspicion or maybe I'm even somewhat paranoid. But no, not at all, I'm experienced and no one's going to cover my ass any better than I will.

    Phil came up escorted by Pete, the girls had a very warm hug and I looked over at Pete as I said, "Have a seat my friend, in it for a dime, in it for a dollar!"

    Me: Ladies have a seat, we're going to have a bit of a chat. Well Phil, your little friend here, in this stunningly gorgeous outfit needs to be schooled on what the uniform of the day needs to be. I trust that you will take care of that. Ladies, you are both here for separate and distinct reasons. We don't want to cross those two up. Amy, you will be sitting here with the group but not participating. Your job will be to observe me, the way I form my words, my sentence structure and my general overall attitude. Monitor my facial structure, my hand gestures and my overall body movements. Having brain scan after brain scan tells you very little about the actual damage that has taken place. All a scan can do is measure the shrinkage of the brain and whether or not there's an active bleed. The reason I want that information is that I want to know when it's time for me to quit. That's quit writing, not quitting life, just writing. I'll be damned if I put out a subpar novel after my past books have been so jokingly unsuccessful. Again Amy your findings are to be only mentioned to me and no one else, is that clear?

    Amy: Yes sir, crystal clear. David could we step away from this topic for a moment and may I ask you a question? Actually it's a question that's being asked by many. We are not the only people who read your work, David. How is it as you just jokingly said unsuccessful writings, how is it that people don't get it?

    Me: People don't get it because they don't want to get it. The world only wants bouquets and wagging puppy dog tails. This same world only wants the truth as long as it is kind and loving. People see the hard truths as cruel and vicious to their comfort. Many, if not most, view the introduction of hard reality as an assault to their sensitivities, as it is a personal affront to their comfort and they resent the hell out of me.

A case in point;

The movie, "A Few Good Men" was a box office smash. I personally applauded it for the reasons that few (damn few) did. Most viewers celebrated the innocence of both the mind and act of the young Marines at the end of the movie. For me it was when Tom Cruise was grilling Jack Nicholson on the stand and Cruise was demanding the truth. After both parties were shouting and spitting through their clenched teeth Nicholson loudly stated, "You can't handle the truth!"

Amy sweetheart, I'm like the guy that goes to an antique store and buys a very expensive, centuries old and very large heavy wooden dining room table. I strip that table of its gorgeous finish with a belt sander and then, run it through a wood planer a few times to make sure that everything is square, I cut it to size and build the most exquisite wooden pallet to put in my shed to keep all the flower pots on during these far too many brutal fucking months of winter. Liken that to my writings and neither make any sense.

Amy girl, a great number of people don't want to get it and yes it frustrates the shit out of me. I look at people who take a picture and they can sell it for a lot of money. Just one photograph will sell for who knows, either a month or six months of a home mortgage. Christ almighty, even a new car perhaps and it took them only minutes! Minutes with very minimal investment other than their equipment costs. They put in minutes maybe just seconds perhaps and they come up with what they consider to be art. Well they didn't build the fucking picture of that bird or those trees or clouds or catch the rainbows. They took a picture. Let's examine the word took. They took something that was already there and made it their own, so isn't that in fact considered to be theft? They so proudly frame those photographs and hang them in a gallery and sell them for a shit pot of money! I have one friend who is a hobby painter and he likes to paint different sceneries, some wildlife but mostly natural stuff in the woods and he just does this shit on parchment paper mounted to poster board. He doesn't frame it, he doesn't do anything with it. He dips his brush tip into some kind of paint and brushes something that he sees and sells it to people as art, supposed art that takes him just a few hours or less to do. Well that's a lot more artful than a guy with a camera granted, but again all you're recording is what you're seeing, you have not created anything! Let's not forget about the movie industry, actors want you to believe that it's their story. It's not their story, they're just telling a story. They're telling the story that was written by a writer who created that story. Those actors want us to believe that they are bringing the story to life. Bullshit, the author gave the story life. Let's remember that that actor is supported by the production company who has hundreds if not even thousands of people involved with unlimited funds for that one movie, when you throw in extras and whatnot. Nothing was founded or developed by the actors or the directors or whoever else is in charge of all that shit. It all came from the mind and hand of a writer. We can take it another step when it comes to music. Who writes songs? Writers write songs, it's true enough that some singers are actually songwriters but most singers buy the songs written by writers and in many cases by other singers who happen to also be writers. Take Stevie Nicks from Fleetwood Mac. Stevie wrote Fleetwood Mac's only #1 song, "Dreams" in just ten minutes, if you believe the publicists and other press agents. So don't come at me with all that original song bullshit stuff. There's nothing original about taking from someone else and calling it your own just because you paid for and formatted it differently!

    Now step away from that and look at what it takes to write just a single fucking book. For me, it's ten to twelve to even fourteen months from beginning, to having the published novel in my hand. There are times that I write two books, side-by-side and publish them a few months apart. All of my books average close to three hundred and thirty pages and close to ninety + thousand words with twelve hours of reading.

    I spend (on average) ten to twelve hours every day writing and that's six days a week. I sell my books for $17.95. Just because I sell them for that price, doesn't mean I'm going to sell them at all. That's just the price, so yeah it's frustrating. Of course I get bummed out, but I have to revisit the core of why I write and I humbly must admit, I write to help others like myself and my writing is also my way of making living amends to people that I adversely affected throughout my lifetime. Simple enough, sweet sister Amy?

Amy: I have no words for that but I have a question. Do all writers go through the same thing?

Me: I don't know, I don't have any writer friends other than Christine Bomey, we share much of the same struggles as do thousands of other Independent authors. Keep in mind that there are hundreds of thousands of writers throughout the world that have written books, but for multiple reasons, have never had their work published. My guess is that many of those lack confidence.

Amy: That I sadly understand, I have to wonder as I often do wonder where I would be today if not for my family's support.

Me: That's wonderful. Now you two, I know how you met, well according to Phil that is, and obviously your bond was struck up because of your fondness for me, is that correct? Both of you girls have told me how you get giddy when speaking of me. Let me give a bit of counsel to the both of you. If you don't have that same gut thing that you both share for me with your boyfriend or whoever the hell it is, I don't even know if either one of you has a boyfriend or I don't know if you're even married but let me stress this. If you don't get that same burn in your belly for the men that you're with, that you have for me, you don't have love, what you have is convenience. Millions upon millions of people are dedicated or married only because of their need to not be alone. You don't have a lover, what you have is a convenient roommate and the emptiness that goes along with that, and at some point it will harm you. I have to go back to Heather's Council when she told a friend of ours who is looking for a life mate, "You first must make friends if you're going to be lovers and you need to be best friends if you're going to be married." Kids, I've lived a complete life of emptiness in my recent past because I didn't know how to win, I just knew how to lose. Today I'm experiencing the win of many many years of failures and I believe my five ex-wives will bear that out. Now this is something I don't want shared with the other part of the group, this is just between us three girls, oh and you of course Pete, not that I'm calling you a girl because I think you could probably stomp a mud hole in my ass, so I want to be nice to you!

Pete just shook his head and slowly smiled.

Ladies, we're going to meet at noon in the private dining area in the restaurant downstairs. So Phil, why don't you take care of Amy's wardrobe and if need be, Pete I trust that you will give the girls a lift to Kohl's or wherever. I don't know where the fuck you go to buy women's clothes. But at lunch time Amy, you will be wearing the uniform of the day. *Capiche?*

I excused the two ladies along with Pete. I then called Doris and I asked her to gather up Marge, Wyatt, Manfred and Abby and I'll meet them at the lobby elevators in ten minutes. As always and I guess this is just my way, they met me at the lobby elevators, all with quizzical looks on their faces. I don't know why I do that to people, I just do that, I don't understand it but yet I do, it's part of my weirdness I guess.

Me: Kids, we're going to run up to the Eagles Nest for just a few minutes. I know you're busy with your stuff but I want to brief you on how I've redesigned part of our structure. I don't want to blind side anyone, I clearly remember you Doris, giving the admonishment you gave me about how we must be a team of oneness, a cohesive unit and shit like that, right?

Once we got to the Eagles Nest I invited everyone to help themselves to refreshments or whatever was in the kitchen as I said, "We're only going to be here for a few minutes. I want you guys to know that I'm bringing in another person to our merry little tribe. That's I, as in me, to assist me in a different venue but she will be observing what goes on in the Eagles Nest or wherever else we meet.

Marge: David don't you find that a bit dangerous, have you vetted this person, how do we know that they're not batting for the other team? I've seen a few Trojan Horses in my career, it never goes well. Can you give us a little more information about this person?

Me: I trust this person implicitly. She is part of my wellness team which has nothing to do with any of you. I understand and I do very much appreciate your concern to protect me but let's remember that this may be your show but this is still my theater.

Marge: Fair enough honey, I guess it has to be, but please be careful.

Me: Thank you sweetheart, I will. Anyone else?

Doris: I heard that you brought in an absolute bombshell of a woman a little bit ago, I have to assume that that's our new person?

Me: That woman isn't just a bombshell, she is wickedly beautiful and no, I don't have eyes for her, she is a professional, no different than any of you. What do you have to say Wyatt?

Wyatt: I just want to look at her and her smile.

Me: Fred, do you have anything?

Frederic: No sir, I'm with Wyatt.

Me: You two swinging dicks best not do anything to make Amy uncomfortable. If you do, I will handle you both, in a very undelicate way. Have either one of you ever been on life support?

Those two young men suddenly sat up as straight as they possibly could and looked away.

Doris: Gentlemen, I know how to handle a chainsaw and a wood chipper. I don't think that David is kidding, I know I'm not. You best take heed.

Me: I don't have any time for this silliness, you lads tuck away your tiny little peckers. Fred, what do you have?

Frederic: We have constructed a rather lengthy list of questions for you and somehow I have this unsettling, spooky feeling. I don't have any information to support it but I have a distinct feeling that this whole thing is going to come together really fast with the opposing team. If it's okay with you I would just like to keep my head down and work through all this so we can be prepared. I think part of their strategy may be to catch us off guard, is that fair David?

Me: Fred, I think we all have that thing in our belly moving around like a swishing cat's tail. Yes it could be any day. Well I like to shoot from the hip, when it comes, if it comes. But yes, preparedness is absolutely paramount, forewarned is forearmed, so let's spend the next few days really banging on this. I don't know how much sleep you people require but you're going to get less than what you're used to, fair enough? If you don't have anything more I don't have anything more, we'll meet in 45 minutes for lunch. Come on, I'll walk you to the elevator and use my magic key to send you boys and gals back to your rooms.

I decided to lay down in the bedroom for a brief nap but not trusting myself, I set the alarm and I'm glad I did. I would have slept right through lunch without question. I privately knew that I had been slipping a little faster than I wanted to admit to myself or to anyone else. I've been knocking around the idea that I might need some level of medication to level me off. I was doing okay with the limited mobility part but I could feel my mind slipping. I'm really hoping that Amy can help me somehow stay focused, I've been feeling a panic that I am running out of time rather quickly. It's strange how it actually mirrors the feelings I get after I finish a book. I have always had to battle with some level of depression throughout my life. Once I complete a writing and there's nothing more to write and when I get to the stage where I have to turn my work over to my friend Angie to have the book formatted, before it's moved on to publishing, I get anxious.

    As with every book I've completed, I feel a deep loss each time. This book has been my all day and late night companion, it holds my fears of failure, It holds my many shames, It's my confidant and my father confessor. I can write about and confess my sins and crimes. If I get even too deep for me, I can simply slap the backspace key and make it all go away. Another bothersome thing is that maybe I was missing something in my rush to publication. I of course fully know what is behind that anxiety. Part of me says, I need to write to stay alive, the other part of me says I need to finish before I die, it's just a very weird thing.

    Once I have Angie submit my book for publication, I get one opportunity to review it and make any final corrections before it goes on to printing. Each and every time I start that, "What if game, what if I miss this, what if I miss that?" I've had some major flaws printed that I can't withdraw. Unless

I'm willing to pay for editing services it will be printed as is. My book size has always been a standard six by nine inch layout with at least three-hundred plus pages and ninety to one hundred and twenty thousand words but it's not just about the numbers, it's about the content of course. I know I have to produce a visual on paper that makes the reader know that they're getting not only a quality book but a value book with a strong page count and a reasonable retail price.

What's been bouncing in my head as of late came from a gentleman from St. Louis that has published several books and is a highly respected contributor to several publishers. He once told me over a phone call that started with, "Let me be candid with you, as an independent novelist you will never find fame on your own, you will never be discovered. Either you're a part of the machine or you're not. If you don't have influence which of course equates to money and political powers, there will never be room at the table for you." He jokingly and part seriously told me, "There's only two ways for a person like you to find fame.

Firstly: If you were to be murdered in a very public fashion with great media coverage and a few cell phone videos on youtube.

Secondly: If you were to murder someone in a very public way with strong media coverage, you would of course be discovered, you would however only be discovered as a killer sitting on death row and nothing more." He gave me several examples of killers who did things in a very public fashion whose names are soon forgotten beyond that 15 minutes of fame. "Fame is not everlasting, death most certainly is!"

Amy was suddenly standing in front of me.

Amy: David I suggest you stop writing, at least for now. You're giving too much of yourself and are receiving far too little in return. It's like you're trying to fill a plastic laundry basket with those cut-outs with water. You'll let that water tap run to the end of time but that laundry basket with all the cut-outs will never fill unless of course you just want to piss away your life with a dream, a dream that even you know that you will never recognize.

Me: Good read young lady. I'm at that very crossroads as we speak, other than feeling that I'm just marking time until I die, I have been asking myself, "What is it all worth, where is the value?" I have become mentally, emotionally and physically exhausted, not to mention my spiritual condition which of course gets put away because I think I've got bigger fish to fry. I forget all about my needs for my conscious contact with the God of my understanding, because I think I have a greater purpose. Well there's an ego that's more than just a bit out of control but if I don't write what else will I do?

There's no question that my mental process is diminishing but what's almost as shocking, is that my advancing vertigo has all but rendered me homebound. I can't even go for a short walk. And with that, I've come to the realization that my days of fishing with my friend Dave Quinn are over. I can't go near any body of water, the moment I do I will lose my equilibrium and find myself in the drink. I've never had a problem with seasickness regardless of the wave action but now, I don't think I could walk well enough just to get down the dock to get in the boat. My greatest joys during the summer months are to go trout fishing along the river banks. I can't trust myself any longer around water or out on the boat with my friend Dave. We troll around Lake Superior trying to scare the trout away. But it was never about the fishing, it was always about being pals. Fishing was our play time, that was when we let go of everything and just both be present, in the present. There were usually three of us on the boat and we teased each other without mercy. We teased each other about all kinds of shit. There was no bitching about spouses or families or jobs, there was no talk of politics. It was just boys being boys. I always felt refreshed when I was out on the big lake and when I came home that day, I had some of the best naps ever. Fresh air and friendship cures a lot of ills but this time, I know it won't clear or cure my ills. Of course our friend Jimmy won't be there this year either, because Jimmy died a few months back. Jimmy coughed through most every meeting for several weeks. We all thought he just had a bad cold and he needed to stay home and take care of himself. For whatever reason, I too am one of them, 'but people' much like my pal Jimmy. In

Minnesota men want to believe that they're going to be just fine, no matter the injury or ailment. Very few males will ever go to see their doctor unless they're dragged there in the back of an ambulance. Jimmy, sadly, was no different than me or the rest of our Pals. Jimmy did get to go for a ride in the back of an ambulance because he was having difficulty breathing. In a week's time Jimmy was told that he had stage four lung cancer. At the end of the third week of his diagnosis our pal Jimmy was in hospice and then of course he passed. If you watch any amount of TV, especially during the daytime, every commercial has to do with whatever symptom you think you might have and suggest that you need to buy their product (operators are standing by) just in case. The over-the-counter industry is completely unregulated, they can make any claim they want which has to do with their remedy being better than any others. They use washed-up celebrities and has-been athletes to hawk their products. Then we have the prescription manufacturer's doing the same but they must do test trials and list the side effects and all of the potential dangers, including death! I don't think I want any of that shit in my body, the side effects are worse than the illness.

So as a consumer, I should be taking medication that just might kill me so I can feel better? What the fuck kind of reasoning is that? Of course the drug manufacturers own our government leaders and you have no chance to recover any kind of damage from the FDA approved bullshit. With most all things in life, everything is about the dollar and only about the dollar. I love it when I hear people speak about how wonderful their doctor is and how he's helping them with this or that. What the doctor is doing is writing prescriptions (that you may not need) to bill your insurance company's and you better know the drugs being prescribed are from the drug company that is paying the doctors the most money to prescribe. All he or she is doing is to fulfill your need to remain quiet and stoned. It's startling when you stop to think about how little doctors actually know. How many false positives and false negatives come out from laboratory work? Everything's a guessing game, nobody wants to spend the time or the money to perfect anything and all you ever hear is, "Here try this, see if this works?" They don't care that it's your body they're talking about, your life and your family's livelihood, they don't care about any of that! You damn well better have a billfold full of money. We see all these many retired professional athletes hocking somebody's medications, what the fuck do they know about that shit? Celebrity endorsements run the gamut from OTC viagra to auto, life and extended auto warranty insurance. Of course, we can't leave out the loving hearts that want to buy your house mortgage so you can have a better life but you can still live in your house until you die. What's the matter, did these guys spend all their money on cocaine and whores that they need to do commercials? The testimonials as to how they improved their sex life is another scam. Their body's have been so saturated with performance enhancing steroids of some type, so of course they're going to have, 'tiny soft weiner syndrome'.

Chapter 17
The Newbie

Our little jaunt to the circus was greatly enjoyed by everyone. It's pretty sad that they took away all the big animals but I get that whole animals in captivity thing but then again, that's all these animals have ever known. You have to wonder how they've adjusted to their new freedom.

We were set to meet Monday morning at 7:00 a.m. in the Eagles Nest. Everyone was on time and looked somewhat refreshed. What I found interesting is that even when Amy is dressed in sweats and a rather loose fitting football jersey she still looks smoking hot. Those two clowns that took the big spanking the other day did their very best not to look at her, I guess that they finally got it figured out.

Me: All right you guys, a little change of plans here. I'm sure you've got plenty of your notes all worked up and you're all just chomping at the bit to come hot out of the chute. For my dime, I think you're all pissing up a rope and with that same rope you're trying to shoot a game of pool. You're off the mark, you are all damn far off of mark so I'm going to bring you back to where we need to be. I know exactly where they're going to go with situations that took place in my life. They're looking for my involvement with anyone that suffered a death whether it be natural or accidental or in some cases suicide. So I'm taking you to chapter #7 titled, "The Deadly Agenda" and perhaps even a bit before that one. Their big questions are going to be, "Is Paul Roberts real, are any of the Roberts family members real, is "The Company real?" My answer is simply going to be, "It's as real as you'd like it to be, I'm a novelist, I write novels."

They'll ask if the Duluth Police Sergeant being murdered was real and if he died at the hands of my friends. I'm sure they're going to ask if I really wasn't there. They will insinuate that I was just lucky to escape. Well that could be a valid question, although I wasn't there when the Patrol Sergeant was murdered by my friend and his cousin. But no, I had no part in that. Let me ask any of you if you knew where you were and what you were doing and with who on a particular date and time, fifty fucking years ago, half of you guys weren't even born yet!

I'm sure they're going to ask about my friend drowning down off of Park Point, when we all were in our early teens. Yes he drowned, no nobody drowned him. I wasn't even there, I was further down the beach with some of the other guys and from there they would want to know about my grandma who I called jiggles because I openly spoke of my hatred for her. Yes she was a hateful bitch but no, I didn't kill her. She died in a nursing home from natural causes which I still to this day, find greatly disappointing. Okay from there to, let's see what else? Oh yeah, then there's my friend Carl Burgel who owned the ambulance service. He died an accidental death. He was storing trusses in the old ambulance garage that he turned into a medical supply store. As Iunderstand, he was rearranging trusses for his new home build to make more room in the rear of the old ambulance hall when the whole group of them fell and crushed him to death. I was living in Colorado at the time, I don't have the dates but I'm sure you can dig those up, I'm sure they will at least.

    Of course, then we can go on to a former father-in-law in Colorado who was my favorite drinking buddy at the time. He died from a massive heart attack while in his vehicle which crashed into the back end of the bar that we were just having drinks in. No, I didn't kill him, he was my buddy.

    The real meat is going to come in this whole deal, is whether or not I murdered Bernie Wayne Jacobs. That's the son of a bitch that murdered my friend, Firestone Town Marshall, Rick Hart. No, I was hundreds and hundreds of miles away but I wish I could have been there. I very much wish I could have put that bullet into his chest. So what if his death was suspicious, who the fuck cares? Fuck him, he needed to be dead. Yeah I know that I gave some smart-ass remarks to the FBI agents about Bernie Jacobs when asked what I was doing a few days before his body was found. I told them that, "I was'nt sure but I was either working, sleeping, fighting or fucking and they could pick one!" The other three guys with me said the same. This whole fucking circus act is nothing but fluff, bluff and bluster. Yes I fully know how people can take something that's nothing and make it to something huge. Now I kind of understand that there won't be a jury seated but there will be a panel of three questioning me? It will be televised and probably end up broadcasted on a number of television and social media networks. Do you know the downside to that? There is none, the upside of that is that I'm going to sell a whole fuck of a lot of my books. I don't know if we have to go any further with any of this. Doris you have the floor, what say you?

    Doris: David I couldn't agree with you more but you have to look at what we're up against. I'm sorry, but we've got to stay on this. We've got to be pragmatic all throughout. We've got to be ready or they'll just steamroll over the top of us. If we get blindsided and we can't produce arguments right off the top, the panel will rule in their favor. We have to have our notes in order, we have to have our answers in order.

    Well David, here's something you might find interesting, I know they will as I do. When you spoke of, I believe it was in, "Harvest Season/Body Parts" on page 130 about Ernest Hemingway and him writing "Baby Shoes" which was only six words on a bar napkin. You made the comment that if you were there at that time, that you would have thrust a steak Knife into his jugular vein. You do know that's awful damning.

    Me: Yeah I guess you could look at it that way, I don't give a fuck either way. I didn't jab a steak knife into his jugular vein but I wish I could have, I would have killed every one of those mother fuckers at that table with their laughing and applauding his brilliance as he wrote of dead babies. You want to talk about a fucking psychopath, start with him. He indiscriminately piled up exotic wildlife bodies with his bloodlust just to kill. Sweetie, keep in mind that he worked on an ambulance during the war as a volunteer. Was he a serial killer, did he kill his patients in the back of that ambulance? Let's play with that question for a bit of time!

    We all know that those cock-licks will take everything out of order and context. They will fuck with all the timelines to confuse you. This ain't your first rodeo and we all know whoever the, 'bought and paid for' judge is, that you're not going to be allowed to object to anything. Even your objections will not be heard, let alone acknowledged. As we have all agreed, this is a fucking witch hunt and nothing more. Believe me when I tell you, I would love to hunt down each and every one of those sons of bitches!

    Amy: People, I'm calling a halt to this session. I understand David's frustration and anger. He's lived through it and now you're putting it right in front of his face so he gets to relive it all over again. I will not allow any of you or the opposition to continue in this manner. *Capiche?*

Please gather your things, this session is over, please everyone leave this office now! Pete, will you do the honors and escort these nice people the fuck out of here and please call for your in-house medical team, stat?

The room cleared like we were at a wedding reception when it was announced, "The bar is now open and the drinks are free!"

I have never heard such a powerful statement with so few words by such a beautiful woman. As a matter of fact, I was a little bit intimidated too! I was almost ready to jump up from my chair and leave with the rest of them.

Me: Amy, what's with the medical team stat thing all about?

Amy: I want to monitor your blood pressures and pulse rates for a few minutes. I saw your left eye start to pulsate and your pupils enlarge. How many fingers am I holding up?

Me: Stop it, you know damn well that I can't see right now. If you call for an ambulance I will dive out of a fuckin window. Blind rage is not just a description, it's a condition. I just need to catch my breath and dump my rage and everything will return to normal. Amy dear, I couldn't be any more grateful than to have you in my corner, but if this kind of stuff continues, I'm going to have to have Heather sit next to me every time we meet. Oh and one more thing before the medical people arrive, you used my favorite word a few minutes ago without my permission but you did use it well, don't do it again. *Capishe?*

    We both laughed as the paramedics arrived. Yes, I knew that the paramedics would be arriving and not hotel security/medical. I caught both of Amy's and Pete's winks and slight head nods as the gang was quickly filing out of my suite. The three paramedics and four firefighters came into my suite, it looked like it was moving day with all the gear they were carrying with them. I laughed as I said, "Folks it's not whatever somebody told you it is. I'm just having a little problem with anxiety and frustration. I'm not on or anywhere near death's door but help yourself to any refreshments and snacks in the kitchen."
    As the Paramedics were hooking me up to a twelve lead heart monitor their eyes were wide with taking in all of the view of both the interior and exterior of my suite.
They all had a slight grin as they went to do their work. I couldn't help but laugh as they tried their damnedest to be professional and remain focused but they kept glancing out the windows, of course. Amy caught it as well as she said, "Ladies and gentlemen, I asked you to come today to monitor my patient's vital signs, he's been through a great deal of stress. If you wouldn't mind hanging around, I'll pay whatever

charges necessary but I would like you to do a blood pressure every five minutes for the next thirty minutes. Is that possible?"

Who I had to assume was the lead firefighter smiled and said, "Ma'am with the offer of refreshments and snacks along with this view, we will sit here all day with you! Do you mind sir if we start an IV, It's just a precautionary protocol?"

Me. Well if I was unconscious I guess I'd say yes but since I'm wide awake and grinning, I think we'll pass on that IV thing. The moment you stick me for an IV you are committed to transport me to the hospital. When I tell you all to go shit in your hats, the nice policeman who I don't see at the moment will 'Baker Act' me and force me to go to the hospital in restraints.

It wasn't another ten minutes and out of nowhere stood Heather. She looked frightened as well as angry but her always being the consummate lady, held herself back but I knew there would be an explosion in due time. Heather looked at Amy and introduced herself, they both had genuine smiles but I could feel the undercurrent, slight as it might be but it was definitely there. It was one of those things when you get two extremely attractive women face to face with deep concern for the same man. Yeah there's going to be a joust of some kind at some point.

After three readings of my blood pressure, everything fell back to normal. So the guy who wants to believe that he has full control of his body and his emotions just shit the proverbial bed. It made me angry, I've always had full control of myself at least ever since I've been sober for the last 32 years and now this bullshit comes out of nowhere? I guess I haven't truly surrendered to the idea that I no longer have full control of my mental and physical movements. As of late, Dementia controls me and I fucking hate it!

Suddenly there's a three-way conversation between Heather, Amy and Pete as to whether or not I should take the ride to the hospital. I smiled as best I could. I was still feeling quite embarrassed about the attention I was getting as I said, "So you three are going to decide my fate? It's not like I've died and you're trying to pick out the perfect Mortuary and are deciding on the flower arrangements! I'm here, I'm right fucking here! I'm a big boy, I'm an emancipated adult and I've been one for some time now, for the fucks sake! I will make my own decisions and no I don't need to go for the ride, the hospital will and can do quite well without me. What I do need is to go home, pet my babies, drink a few gallons of Folgers coffee and smoke a couple packs of cigarettes, before the sun goes down.

After the 4th blood pressure reading I was startled to look over and see (maybe I smelled her before I saw her) but I somehow knew that she was there. She may have been there for some time for all I know, there was an awful lot of commotion around me but there it was, that scent, that same scent that I picked up in the Seafarer Room a few days back. That faint scent of a lost love from many, many years ago. Poor Alana was standing there looking like she may need some medical attention herself. Alana and I had made amends a couple years back and really haven't had much to say with each other since. She's the hotel manager here and has been for some time, she's been quite successful. I said hello to her and once again, there's two women looking at a third woman who is equally as attractive as the other two, this whole thing is going to get me killed. Heather had met Alana before and of course I told Heather about Alana from the many years back, it's actually been decades before Heather and I came together. Alana reached out and gave Heather a hug and whispered something to her. They had a brief back and forth whispered conversation. The only thing I picked up from all that was Heather saying, "I'll ask him, I'll call you later today."

Chapter 18
The Interview

Later that day after the rescue circus left, I went home. I was sitting on my back deck deeply into my second pot of Folgers coffee and I was not about to slow down when the doorbell rang and Heather answered it. She brought out a package from the pharmacy. It had some prescriptions from my doctor and a pulse oximeter that you put on your finger to measure both heart rate and blood oxygen levels.

Me: Honey what's this stuff? I didn't ask for anything, I didn't even talk to my doctor.

Heather smiled and she said, "Baby I talked to your doctor and you better slow your roll with that whole thing about you're in charge of you. I'm in charge of you, do I have to bring out the notarized paper that says that you've given me full medical authority when it comes to your care and wellness. I call the ball, you can bully all those other people all you want down at the hotel but not in this house, I run this show, can you dig it? Oh excuse me, let me rephrase that. *Capiche*?

As long as I have your attention I need to inform you that you'll be doing an interview tomorrow morning with a very sweet seventeen year old high school senior and you are going to be a perfect gentleman, you are not going to embarrass that child with your filthy language and snide remarks."

Me: Woman, I hired you as a wife not my business manager, you don't get to schedule shit when it comes to my time and my work!

Heather: Are you really willing to die on this hill? I just told you that you have an interview to do in the morning and you will be a perfect gentleman and I'll be here to make sure of it.

Me: Okay boss, who is this delightful child that I'm supposed to meet and do an interview with?

Heather: Well darling, it's your old flame's daughter, Avery. She seems to have taken a liking to you from your writing but as I understand it, she's much like sweet old Granny, it seems that they both take great exception to your filthy language in your writings.

Me: So what is this kid, a school newspaper reporter, what's the deal with her?

Heather: Well sweetheart, Alana and I have gotten to know each other over the last several months, yeah she's my embedded snitch and you're going to do her daughter a favor because you're a nice man, you asshole! Now enough of that, what would you like for dinner?

    Me: How about a heaping serving of humble pie? All of you bossy women are going to kill me, you know that right?

    At 9:30 the following morning, Alana and her daughter, Avery arrived at the house. Heather told me the night before that she thought that having a meeting in the 'Eagles Nest' would be too distracting for a young lady, so she decided that we would meet at our house. I don't know why it is, but every time Heather advises me of a decision she's already made without my giving any input, it still fires me up. I can almost feel my blood pressure building, I'm still a free man God damn it! When are people going to learn to respect that? The short answer, probably never!

    Poor Alana's daughter looked like she was going to explode. She has a timidness about her, it doesn't match her mother's persona or her mother's beauty. She's a real simple looking kid, kind of like a little house on a prairie child, what was her name? Laura Ingalls or something like that, I don't know. I sat her down directly across from me as I said, "Young lady, I have some basic rules that you need to understand and respect before we start.

    Rule number one: Don't write anything that I didn't tell you. You can have your opinion but don't quote me unless I'm quotable, got it?

    Rule number two: When I say the word 'pass' that means that I am not going to answer your question. If I say 'pass', that young Miss, means it's time to move on to the next question. A number of people like to push forward once they hear the word 'pass', however those are the people that I excuse at that very moment and will never be allowed to return.

Okay now, what can I do for you young lady? Oh and one other thing, please do not refer to me as Mr. Brown or Sir, my name is Dave. Please call me Dave, let's have it Avery, what's this meeting all about?

Avery: Well Sir…

I waved my pointer finger in front of her. "It's Dave sweetheart, it's Dave. Please call me Dave, take a breath and start over.

Avery: Well Dave, I'll have trouble with that. I have never referred to an adult by their first name, ever. My mother taught me quite well to respect my elders.

I glanced over at Alana and she just grinned. I nodded and said, "Nice job Mom, now let's move on.

Me: Avery, what's up with your bad self?

Avery: Well David, I, I want to be a writer and I've read everything that you've written and I really like your style. I've wanted to meet with you for the last year or so but my mom kept telling me that now is not the time, so I've had a lot of time to prepare my questions.

Me: Take another long deep breath sweetheart. Rather than talking about your questions, tell me your questions. Let's have it, what are your questions?

Avery: My greatest question is and I don't want to embarrass you but my question is, why aren't you famous?

Me: Avery my dear, that's the $50,000 question. Sweetheart you're not the first and I'm sure you won't be the last to ask that question. The best way I can answer that for you is, because I don't care, I don't care if I'm famous, none of that matters to me. So let me ask you, why do you think I should be famous?

Avery: David, I've been reading since I was a small child and I think you're the best writer that there's ever been, but maybe I'm a little bit prejudiced, but you help people! You don't just write books, you write loving messages to total strangers and you give people hope. Who else does that, I don't think anybody, at least not in the way that you do. I'm a Facebook friend of yours and I read some things that you write and the things that people respond to and I'm just sitting here amazed. As a matter of fact, if I may, I'd like to read from my notes.

Me: Yes sweetheart, go ahead.

Avery: Well, you wrote something just four days ago on Facebook that said and I quote; "There's nothing more emotionally satisfying than receiving a message from a reader that says I made a difference in their life." David people went nuts with that! You had over 200 likes and sixty comments! I'd like to read a few of their comments.

Sally wrote, "You words speak straight to my heart because I've never read anything like them, I've been through a lot. Please keep writing and I'll keep reading!"

Lori wrote, "I totally agree, I love this man!"

Jim wrote, "Dave you made a difference in my life just by helping me to reach out."

Tammy wrote, "You've made a vast difference in my life, you'll never know how appreciative I truly am."

Gail wrote, "Outstanding, you have made a difference in my life and many others."

Patricia wrote, "Totally agree, David you have a great insight into humanity, please keep going David!"

Me: Young lady, yes I am moved by my facebook friends and my loyal readers' statements, but where the hell are you going with all this. We are not going to go all day here and we will not be having a sleepover telling scary stories.

Avery: Can you not feel the power that you have and what you do for others? Many of these people are total strangers! David, here's an email I found that reads, "Good afternoon, I just got done reading, "Daddy Had to Say Goodbye", it was an emotional book to read. I teared up many times regarding the things you had to go through growing up. My heart was hurting as I read it. I admire you for the man you have become. I wish I had someone in my life like you. You overcame so many obstacles in your life. I'm happy to be able to call you a friend. I had many things to overcome in my life too but I made the best of it. Take care of my friend David, you are a man who has the ability to change other people's lives by writing a book. You taught me that acceptance and change is an inside job."

    Me: Sweetheart, all I can do is tell my story and hopefully it'll help others dare to tell their own story. It's about freedom sweetie, it's about being who you can be without fear of reprisal or being judged harshly. Yeah there's a bunch of fuckers in this world and I'm not going to apologize for my using that word. People oftentimes carry such a deep level of jealousy that their only hope for normalcy or at least it's appearance is to destroy other human beings, so that they don't look bad. Yeah that's pretty fucked up all right but it's one of our many realities that are very unpleasant to deal with. So let me ask you this, what are your future plans, what do you want to be when you grow up?

    Avery: Well sir, I mean David. I would like to be maybe a journalist. I know I could never be as good a writer as you and I could never even dream about being a novelist.

    Me: Stop, stop with your bullshit and stop it now! You claim that you've read all of my books and yet you've learned very little. So here you sit in front of me, the man who you greatly admire and you demean yourself? That my child is not acceptable, let me ask you this, (as I glanced over at her mother) when you were a child did you ever have to stand in the corner for misbehaving? Avery said yes. I said, "Good, we're about to revisit your childhood. Avery get on your feet, go over to that corner over there and you stand with your nose right in that goddamn corner and you stay there until I tell you, when you can come back out. Take off your sweater and hand it to your mother. I want you to listen to this and you best listen hard!

Nobody can limit your abilities any greater than yourself. I want you to think about one of my favorite statements, "Fear is not a word, at least not in my vocabulary. Fear is simply an acronym which stands for; False Evidence Appearing Real." You're buying off on someone else's bullshit that you're not good enough. How can you ever succeed with that type of mentality? Sometimes we are our own worst enemies and our own worst critics. There are people that want to destroy me because I don't fit their agenda or they're frightened or what the fuck who knows what. I don't give it much thought. So now youngster, your mother, my wife and I are going to go out to the deck and enjoy the sunshine. You stand right where I told you to, until I release you.

Avery was sobbing a bit and I thought that was okay. Not only was that okay but I think we may have just had a possible breakthrough. We three adults went out on the deck and now I've got two women looking at me like I'm a fucking monster for deflating that child and I just smiled and said, "I'm not crushing her dreams, I'm helping her build her dreams, stay out of it, both of you." Of course the two ladies kept glancing inside the house and constantly checking their watches.

    Alana: David, I would like to bring my daughter her sweater. It's cold in your house and she only has a short sleeve t-shirt on.
    Me: Alana honey, either you trust me or you don't. I want her to feel the chill. I want her to cry. I want her to get weak in the knees and start to develop a sore back from standing in one place. I want her to see nothing in that corner but her own unwarranted fears. Leave her be, she is in session. Mom, there will be a time in her life when you won't be able to be there for her. I have to think that you want her to have her own strength at that time. What say you?
    Alana: I understand what you are doing, I hate you at this moment as I am sure my daughter does. Our love for you goes deep, so deep that we understand that you are trying to help us both. Message received, you bastard.

    I knew I had to stay the course even with these two adult women. They had to know that I was in charge and their opinions needed to be kept to themselves. So I waited probably 25 minutes with that sweet poor girl standing in the corner like a small child shivering in punishment. I started to get up and I said, "Ladies I'd like you to remain out here. Avery doesn't need to be rescued, she needs to be saved, saved from herself, saved from her fears, saved from her own low self-image and whatever the hell else is going on in most 17 year old's worlds." I went to the back bedroom and released the dogs from their kennels. They were quite happy to be free. I then went into the kitchen and said, "Avery turn around, punishment is now over but that can return at any moment that you cross me! *Capiche?"*

I had her sit on the couch and told the dogs to say hello. Those little guys were all over her, it was nothing but kisses, kisses and more kisses. Avery was giggling in just a few short moments while petting the kissing dogs. I went out to the deck and said, "Ladies now you're out of punishment, go see the dogs. I don't want anyone to leave until I return." I grabbed my truck keys and went for a quick spin to clear my head and my own tears. As I drove I was thinking of this poor young girl watching her daddy die from cancer at such a young age. When I got back, the girls were just finishing lunch.

Me: Avery, I'm not going to ask you what you learned today but I do hope that you did learn something. She smiled with saying, "Yes sir, I definitely learned something today, thank you.

Me: Okay tell me now young lady, what spawned this whole thing about you wanting to meet with me and write about me, to what your high school newspaper? Is that what this is all about?

Avery: Yes in part, but I also think I wanted to meet you just to say that I've met you, just to tell my friends that I actually got to meet you.

Me: Well we certainly did that, do you need me to write a note or something for your friends and classmates?

Avory laughed as she said, "My mom said I shouldn't do this but, (as she gave me the finger) I hope you don't get mad at me for this."

Me: Honey back to my question, playtime is over and yeah that was really cute by the way. What other reason inspired you to want to meet me?

Avery: David do you know the name Linda Greenlaw?

Me: What's with this shit? So you watched last week's episode of 'Deadliest Catch' the same as I did? This is really interesting sweetie. I had no idea who Linda Greenlaw was until that episode last week. When she was doing her interview towards the end of the show, she gave her Bio and made mention that she's a self-taught author and never had any level of desire to write anything until she told her story to the show's producers and then they wanted her to come onto the show. Well let's get back to the definition of what a publicist does. Publicists build stories, they build back stories, to sell the main story. How much of all of her stuff is actually true? I'm well aware that she's a college graduate. She has a degree in English and was also in law school. Now is she still a self-taught author? She's definitely a legit fisher woman or as she likes to refer to herself as, "A fisherman." I don't have time for that silliness but yeah, she's the real deal. She claims that she was contacted by a publisher via the show producer. Well, with just a bit of research I found she has authored ten to twelve novels and even a few cookbooks. Supposedly her books are all best sellers. With just a bit more research, I found out that she's worth over five million bucks! When did she knock down that five million dollars? Did she have that before or after she started writing? Yeah so she's on the New York Times bestseller list, the real question is not how did she get there but more importantly, who put her there and at what cost? You may think I'm cynical but I'll tell you what I have experienced as a published author. There's a certain level of heartbreak in writing and publishing novels as an independent and not having any true level of success other than the few people who did send me notes of kind words and encouragement and telling me that yes, I did make a difference in their lives. I can't and never will take credit for changing anyone's life, that's God's job. I can only take partial credit for helping them want to change their lives.

    I excused myself and went to my office and wrote with a wide bladed sharpie on a blank sheet of copy paper as I hollered down the hall to Avery, "Sweetheart, how many doors inside and out do you have in your house? How many bathrooms do you have in your house, where do you spend the most time in your house?"

From her information I pushed the button for 30 copies. When they were done printing, I walked back out into the living room and asked Avery, "How many organizations do you belong to in your high school?"

Avery: I don't belong to any groups or organizations other than the National Honor Society, I have had a 4.0 average since the first grade. I don't do any sports either.

Me: Sweetheart, my only claim to fame when it comes to school was in my senior year, when the yearbook staff voted me most likely to do hard-time before turning of age. So how do you interact with your fellow students?

Avery: I really don't talk to anyone and nobody talks to me. I've heard them refer to me as the geek or the freak from time to time, but no one really talks to me.

Me: Well baby, all that's about to change. I know that you attend Denfeld High School and in another nine days, it's going to be career day? Well honey, I'm going to be your guest for career day but I'm not going to just address your homeroom classmates, nope. We will be in the auditorium for an all class assembly. I will speak to the entire student body including your teachers and administrators. Oh and just so you have time to prepare. You, my friend, are going to be on the stage with me. You will have ten minutes to speak of yourself and your journey.

The title of your speech is: "The ghost who steps from my locker."

You will then introduce me as a nine time published author who is mentoring you as you are in the process of writing your first novel titled, "The Ghost Who Steps From My Locker."

That's right baby girl, you have nine days to prepare to speak of your book. I will help you to write your book along with your mom. Honey, you have been living like a ghost ever since you were twelve years old, when your father died.

You girls need to get out of here now. I need my wife to tuck me in, it's time for my nap. Honey these copies all read the same:

"TODAY I WILL CELEBRATE MY LIFE!"

Now give me a hug and get the hell out of my house. I collected hugs from mom and daughter. As Heather was about to open the door for them to leave, I reached into my pocket and pulled out a full dispenser of scotch brand tape as I said, "Avery catch, no excuses, tape those copies in your hand up the moment you get home, to both sides of every door in your house. Every mirror, the refrigerator, stove, TV and everything else you look at."

After they left, Heather sat quietly in her chair but her fingers were flashing as she was tapping the keys on her cell phone. She does like to play a few games on her phone to decompress at times. The look on her face told me something entirely different however. Knowing her as I do, I knew not to interrupt.

She slowly set down her cellphone and looked up at me with a full grin and twinkling eyes.

Me: Do I dare ask?

Heather: You roughed-up that lovely child pretty good. Full grown adults would have crumbled to your asshole attack. She's just a baby you fucking barbarian! Now you're going to pay! I just booked a weekend in Las Vegas for next weekend. Alana, Avery and I are going to fly out on Friday afternoon, we will have a spa day on Saturday and on Sunday, we all are going to have make-overs followed by a mother-daughter clothing shopping spree that may just bankrupt you! That's right bully-boy, I'm using your credit card. You just may have to find a job stocking shelves at Quick-Trip, you fucking Ogre.

Me: Swell, what's for dinner?

Chapter 19
Tire Marks

I had planned on taking the entire weekend off. I didn't care if I did anything or didn't do anything, I just didn't want to do what I've been doing. I'm tired of those people, I'm tired of thinking about those people, I'm just fucking tired!

Well the operative words are, "I had planned." Avery and her mother Alana slapped me on the ass, like a high schooler in gym class with a wet towel. I've been taking too much for granted, thinking that I still have time. Thinking this is not a big deal, thinking, thinking, thinking, but my thinking is not working. I know I've got to get in the game and stay there so of course, I called Doris.

Me: Doris my dear heart, do you have any plans for this weekend?
Doris: Nope just working, sitting right here, just working.

Me: Doris, have you ever been to a drag race? Have you ever heard all the noise, seen a burnout with all the smoke and the big black tire marks on the pavement from racing slicks? Well honey, we're going to a drag race and we're going to make a lot of smoke with burning tires and put down some heavy, heavy rubber. It'll take place in the Eagles Nest at 6:00 a.m. tomorrow morning, tell your pals to all be there. We have been burning daylight, baby. See you in the morning, if you need anything give me a call.

I called Alana and told her I wanted her to bring Avery to the hotel at 6:00 in the morning. I wanted them to briefly sit in with our crew.

I slept well that night even though I was feeling a bit anxious but yet my exhaustion took over and I felt rested. Our dogs seemed to need a bit more attention this morning, so I called Pete and asked him to escort everyone up to the Eagles Nest.
When I arrived everyone was there with their stacks of papers. My only thought was, they have been working damn hard but it's not the time to be rewarded or even complimented, it's time to put our heads down and burn rubber.
I introduced Alana and Avery to the group. There of course were puzzled looks but I pretty much ignored them as I instructed everyone to turn their chairs away from me. All I wanted to see was the back of people's heads. I looked over at Pete and he

brought down a large flat screen from the ceiling. With another nod of my head, Pete queued up the audio of, "I who have nothing" by Tom Jones. I didn't put the lyrics on the screen, I didn't put anything on the screen. I just wanted them to listen to the song but it wasn't Tom Jones singing it. Once the song was over, I explained who Mary Burns was.

    I then had Pete play the full audition video from, "The X Factor" with Mary Burns from Ireland. Mary was a cash register operator in a grocery store where she'd been running the same cash register for 11 years. When she came on stage for her audition in 2010 she looked like a frumpy middle aged woman who wore a home fixed hair style. There was obviously no professional hair stylist or make-up artist involved. Mary wore a very plain looking black V-neck loose fitting smock top with baggy black slacks. No glam bullshit, just flat shoes with no bling. It was just her, it was just fifty year old Mary Burns from somewhere in Ireland, who had a dream to be on, "The X-Factor." As you will see the four judges pretty much blew her off due to her appearance and age. I want you to listen again to Mary singing this song and the panelists' reactions and opinions. Understand this people, Mary Burns walked away from singing several years ago because she lost her faith, she didn't think she was good enough as she suffered from a low self-image. Well, Mary came on stage and blew everyone away, she took a very difficult song and hit it 100%. The judges along with the audience lost their minds as you will see. Mary got the greatest reviews of the

THE GHOST IN OUR LOCKERS

night. Watch her tremble after she finished the song and before the judges spoke. It was the purest of all displays of humility as she wondered if she was good enough. Mary did not just sing a song that night, she sang her life! Mary signed a recording contract with Sony studios that very night!

Sadly, it was the last time that anyone saw the raw, unrefined and angelic Mary Burns. The glitz people swept her up like a Condor snatches up a newborn lamb. She went on to become a very big deal. They restyled her hair, they did all the makeup and wardrobe stuff, along with a dietitian and a personal trainer. Mary lost a great deal of weight and gained the confidence she always longed for. Mary has been on tour for the last thirteen years, enjoying her fortune and hard fought for fame. Two months ago Mary was involved in a traffic accident that almost cost her her life. She is recovering from severe arm and spinal injuries.

The reason I invited my friends, Alana and her lovely daughter, Avery, is that I wanted you all to personally see what a dream in progress looks like. You lawyer people wield great powers. You can support a person's dreams or you can crush those same dreams. The people that you're going to represent during your lifetimes are people with dreams, sadly many will have shattered dreams and broken hearts.

Without the X-Factor, Mary would have died working a cash register as she had no outlet for her dream. Yes, "The X-Factor" was designed as a money maker venture of course for the producers but they do take people along who have the raw talent and better develop them. That's your job, if you're going to be leaders anywhere in this nation under whatever banner you fly. Your job is to serve the people, not yourself, not your buddies. This is not about the weekly sit down $10,000 a plate fundraising dinners. This is about the people, the people that voted for you, the people that believed in you, the people that hope you're going to help their families become stronger and more secure and keep their jobs more secure. That's who you have to serve but believe me when I tell you this. There is a youthful Mary Burns sitting at this table as I speak. There is perhaps another Mary Burns just down the block, who knows maybe even in this very building. These are people with dreams but who don't have the confidence or outlet to pursue their dreams. Your job is to prop people up and to show them that they have a right to believe in themselves. You got that kids?

Now I am taking our lovely guests for ice cream and you lawyer folks need to get to work. I will leave you all with a question that you can only answer within yourselves.

How mighty is your sword?

The ice cream and the company of Alana and Avery made all things in life seem brighter and more wholesome.

When I returned to the Eagles Nest, everyone appeared to be relaxed and refreshed. There were warm smiles and head nods.

Amy: The way you told the Mary Burns story was stunningly magnificent. We all will revel in it throughout our lives and we will share it with many. You missed your true calling by not adding high school and college commencement speaking to your resume.

Me: Thank you. Let's get back to business. Okay who wants to be first? Doris, you're the leader of this pack, you want to start out?

Doris: Yes, I will, thank you. David, we've picked up a few rumors from the opposing team. You, as well as us, know that there's always going to be a leak, sometimes there's even a mole implanted. We have people looking into that but we've got nothing concrete at this point, but we're hopeful.

I already had a pretty good idea of how this whole hearing thing or whatever the fuck this thing it's called, was going to go down.

Doris: In a lot of cases, especially when there's dirtbags on the panel, they will initially come in soft to whoever is in the hearing. So what they're going to do is speak of you like you're all but a Saint. They'll want whoever's hearing this case to feel like they would want to erect a statue of you in your honor. As they go on, that copper-plated statue will fade and turn to various shades of green, covered in pigeon shit. By the time they're done with you, that statue will be pulled down and be dragged down the streets behind a pick-up truck and destroyed. That's their end game, they have to destroy you before you destroy them.

Now we left off with your book, "Flesh of a Fraud" so it's time to move on to your third book, "Altered Egos." Yes, we've all read it, we all have our notes about it, but one of the things that stands out more than anything else in that entire book, besides your kindness and interaction with people who truly needed a friend, is your rage with bad people. The only thing that the opposing team will pull out of that writing is the number of times that you've made statements about you hurting them and you enjoying it, they will follow with you wanting to kill bad guys. That theme runs like a deep river all throughout your writings and you know that they're going to paddle up and down that river with your murdering rants. Of course, we will attempt to counter every claim they make but again, I fear that we won't be allowed to be heard. Even with their accolades of your goodness you must know that this is not about praise, this is strictly about burying you. Although you've had many interactions with people that we may define as deeply troubled and perhaps even broken, we will key on the college professor from the Main U of Minnesota. Her character name is Meredith, I believe. So let me ask you. Is there truly a Meredith character or person?

THE GHOST IN OUR LOCKERS

Me: Well let's step back to where we first started. Would you like the character Meredith to be real?

Marge: Damn it David, you can't play with us like this! We have to know, we have to know if we can interview these people. I don't know if we're allowed to bring in character witnesses yet, but she would be at the top of my list! We need the answer David, is she real?

Me: Yes, yes she's real, as a matter of fact so is her daughter. Now listen to me damn it! In your heart's and in your minds along with my readers, and myself, we all need to believe in the goodness of mankind. Again, I'm a writer, I tell stories. What percentage is true, what percentage is fiction lies within the mind and hearts of the readers. What kind of writer would I be if I told you what you needed to believe and what you need to think and what you need to value?

Phil: David throughout this book, "Altered Egos" you write about your distaste of bad guys, punks and criminals. You admitted in almost all of your books to you wanting to hurt people and in several cases, you admitted to actually hurting people. Followed by your saying how much you greatly enjoyed hurting them! They may try to turn this into some kind of hateful, racist, vigilante behaviors. You may be asked to answer for that. What would your answer be?

Me: Oh, finally something easy. I won't belabor the whole thing about white, straight males being attacked from all sides by the television freak shows and all forms of media. It suddenly seems that the television commercial people have completely run out of white, straight, males for their commercials. Here's what I think. I think our prisons need to be full, I also think we need more prisons. Let's understand that racism comes in all colors and further keep in mind that white is also a color. Racism lives and breathes in the belly of haters, the majority of those haters are actually minority members or minority sympathizers. The why of that silliness lives because it gives them some kind of a perceived positive mainstream identity or so they think. I'd like to tell those phony bastards that I'm not racist and I can prove it, as when I open a pack of Oreo cookies. There's white on the inside but dark brown on both the top and bottom. So you see, I'm not racist at all! I will eat that cookie equally, fuck them losers. Yes of course, there's more people of color in prisons than white people in prison. It's quite easy to understand. More people of color create more crimes than white people. Do this, kids, google St. Louis County Jail Roster, St Louis County, Minnesota. What you're going to find are mugshots of all the inmates currently in custody. A vast number of those inmates are there on hold for DOC warrants which means they violated parole or conditions of their probation, which further means they are repeat offenders or career criminals but fear not, the libtards will throw open the cell doors and tell them to go home and be good boys and girls. Just look at the tattoos on many of their necks and faces. What is their message? Their message screams of hatred for all of society. Since we're on the topic of tattoos, let's examine the purpose of tattoos even for the general public. What's the purpose of permanently marking your body for the rest of your life? As I see it, people want to advertise their uniqueness. They need for whatever reason, to be recognized. Here's a case in point:

    I had a friend who I no longer associate with that is sleeved out with tattoos on both arms that run down to his fingernails. On the back of each hand he has large tattoos of Christ, but this same guy sits and listens to rap music where the artist is singing about raping women, raping children, dismembering women and children and yet he proclaims to be a man of God, dedicated to God to the point where he has God's pictures tattooed on his chest and several other religious symbols. What the fuck does rape and murder have to do with professing his love for God? Yeah, there's some insanity going on there for sure. If you recall, I earlier suggested that if any of you have visible tattoos that you cover them while in my presence. If you need so badly to display who you are but can't speak the words of who you claim to be, you are not who you claim to be. Not all tattoos tell the truth!

    Then we can move on to the tramp stamps which I understand has somehow gone off to the wayside in the last few years. When these women started to age and that tattoo around the upper portion of their hips dropped and became a part of their ass, how disappointing that must be! Then you have the fellas that get tattoos with their girlfriends or wife's names over their heart, on their arm, wherever they put them but here's what people don't understand. Tattoos are permanent, life is temporary. So now this poor fool for whatever reason ends up divorced and gets remarried, what is the message to the new girlfriend or wife? The message is, "There was someone before you." Who the fuck wants to look at that shit? You're telling your mate that they are number two! Class right, total fucking class.

    Now let's get back to law enforcement. Some people want to believe that law enforcement harasses and picks on minorities, nothing could be further from the truth! Understand this, kids, police officers don't have the authority that you may think they do. Their authority is granted to them by the mayor, the sheriff and the state Attorney General's office. Look at the riots that took place here in Duluth. Like everywhere else, the media enjoys reporting that these insane acts of terror were mostly peaceful protests, when they assault civilians, burn buildings and cause everyday law-abiding people to hide in their own homes. What the fuck is peaceful about that? The general public is so fearful of these lunatics that gun sales have gone up exponentially. The price of handguns and ammunition has more than doubled just in the last year from all the panic buying of people knowing that no one's going to protect their family other than themselves due to defunding the police efforts and cowardly elected and appointed officials.

Now there's a fucking model for democracy wouldn't you say?

Jesus Christ, a group of protesters blocked the freeway here in Duluth and the cops stood by and watched and did nothing but it's not on the cops back, it's on the mayor's back. The mayor gives the orders. if you were to interview the cops and ask them why they didn't take action, they probably wouldn't even tell you the truth, the truth is that they feared for their jobs. If they took appropriate and reasonable action, every one of those asshats that were protesting and blocking streets and the interstate that day, would have their asses hauled off to jail. Cops avoid arresting people of color for fear of being labeled as racist, so oftentimes people of color who are committing crimes go unpunished. They don't even get a citation or get arrested. The officers fear retribution from command and the mayor's office which renders them ineffective for the most part. How would you like to live in that high-speed blender of wickedly spinning blades?

Criminal Justice is a term that doesn't fit anywhere in our society today. We the people have become victims of our trusted servants and the end game is always the same, the popular vote. As we all know, the Democrats have gutted our system of justice and now the cops look around and grimace with the thought that Justice actually stands for.... 'Just Us'.

It's really that simple, but the true numbers of people of color and the crimes they commit are whitewashed (pun intended) with all of the sanctuary sympathizers and "Safe Harbor" cities and churches, and you know what I think about churches. If you're going to harbor a criminal from Justice then you too need to be held accountable and I think every fucking church, regardless of the denomination, needs to pay their fair share in taxes like any other business and organization.

I'm sure more than a few of you are looking at what I'm saying as just more conspiracy theory rhetoric. Well, that's your opinion but it's not the truth. My friend Ralph, actually a guy that I grew up with from the old neighborhood posted something like this on Facebook a few days ago and I think that it will give you the true overview of what our country's leaders are trying to do to us;

"If you put 100 black ants and 100 red ants in a jar nothing will happen. But if you shake the jar hard enough, the ants will start killing each other. The red ants will consider the black ants their enemies. The black ants will consider the red ants their enemies. The real enemy is the one who shakes the jar. The same thing happens in human society, so before we attack each other we should think about who is shaking the jar!"

I want you people to think about that statement long and hard. Are we the ants and if so, what color are we and does it truly matter because we're all going to fight to the death. There will be none of us left, choose your sides wisely my friends. With that kids, I'm going for a stroll. Pete, let's roll.

We walked for a couple of blocks and returned to the hotel. I sent Pete ahead because I wanted to make a stop and have a private conversation. I stepped into Alana's office. She was on the phone but motioned for me to have a chair. So I did the only adult thing that I could think of. I pulled both of those overstuffed high-backed chairs together so they were facing each other and I made a little bed for myself and laid down. I couldn't see her now because of the armrests, but she was giggling as she was trying to talk business.

Alana: Thank you for your silence while I finished up with this call. Now would you kindly get your feet off of my furniture and what the hell do you think you're doing just barging into my office?
Me: A few questions babes. Where's your daughter going to go to college? Alana: She's not, she vacillates between wanting to be a professional Writer or a Veterinary Tech. She just loves animals, I know I can swing those costs but College no. I'm sure she could get a scholarship but at the same time I'm being selfish. I don't want to give her up, not for four or six or eight years or even a day. David, she is my baby and my anchor. She gives me purpose, I need her as much as she hopefully needs me. The loss of my husband and her

father made us both isolate, we locked our doors on the world.

Me: Well here's a new game coming to town, sit up straight and listen. This company that you work for has luxury resorts all over the world. It just so happens that they have a luxury resort in the Foothills outside of Fort Collins, Colorado. Colorado State University is located in Fort Collins. CSU is a fully accredited college but their specialty is animal husbandry! Stay with me on this, your company plans on opening petting zoos at a number of their resorts. They're looking for intelligent young people who have a passion for caring for animals and teaching the public about the animals. That's where your daughter is going to go to college. She needs to apply in the next two days. She's already been accepted, her four-year program and her extended program for veterinary school is prepaid, living expenses included. As for you sweetheart, one of the resorts nearby would like to offer you a position as a general manager. Now can I put my feet back on your fucking furniture?

Alana: I don't know what to say. This all is so sudden. I suddenly have a raging headache, none of this can possibly be happening.

Me: Why can't it? Who's more deserving? Part of what I do in my life runs parallel to some of the Roberts family's passions. We both inspire to help others aspire, dig it? No your daughter is not a project, no one's going to look for results. She just needs to stay in school and of course work part-time in the petting zoo. Honey, I do understand your daughter's loneliness from losing her father at such a young age. Tell me about the relationship between her and your husband and her daddy.

    Alana: Damn it David, it's just too early in the day for all this. This is too much to handle, I'm not a drunk but I sure as hell could use a drink right now!

    Me: Hey, I know a guy who runs a place that has drinks, it's just down the hall a little ways. It's before legal operating hours but what do you say we go and imbibe?

    I enjoyed a fresh cup of Folgers coffee and Alana had two drinks of some kind. I don't even know what the hell they were but I could see her start to physically relax. I'm thinking, "Oh shit, here it comes, first the trembles, then the runny nose and the tears and Jesus Christ will there ever be an end to this? I sure picked a hell of a time to live sober!

    Me: Have one more drink and I will have Pete park your car in the security garage and give you a ride home. When you get home, sit down with your little girl and ask her to tell you about her daddy as best she remembers him. As a matter of fact, take one of your voice recorders with you because that's going to be the start of her book and her speech to the student body next week.

    Give me a hug sweetie, I've got to get back to work and when I get to my office, I'm going to put my

DAVID J BROWN

feet all over the goddamn place, who knows, I just might find a way to make footprints up on the ceiling!

Chapter 20
Tire Smoke

    Me: It's time to move on to book #4, "Harvest Season Body Parts." I'll just tell you what the books are about and we can move on to the next because I know where the meat of all this lies and so do you, or at least you should know. So, let's just briefly get through, "Harvest Season Body Parts."

    This is a straightforward examination of why we surrender and why we fail and why success is so difficult. This whole thing is one massive internal mind game. 'Harvest Season' is simply about fears and how we as people empower our fears to control us. We don't want to take responsibility in case we fail, we know we can't blame others in some situations, so we just lay down to our fears and let them have their way with us and we do nothing. We simply exist as we go about our basic day-to-day bullshit.

    Wyatt: David, this is the first time I came to the realization that it's your picture on the covers of most of your books, other than "Daddy Had to Say

Goodbye!" I didn't catch that right away, what gave you away with 'Harvest Season' was the surgical mask and cap, it brought me to focus on your eyes and that was quite startling. You must know that there's a part of me that says those eyes look to be dangerous, at least dangerous, if not even deadly! Even the feel of that book cover kind of gave me the creeps. It's not shiny gloss like all of your other books. It has this waxy filmy stuff that when you pick it up to look at it, you look at your fingers to make sure you didn't transfer anything from the cover.

    Knowing that you never do anything by accident, I have to say that was absolutely brilliant. I picked up that book and I got chills before I even looked at the cover or read anything on the front or back. You have the uncanny ability to change your eye structure and depths. At times I see your eyes with warmth and caring with great compassion. Other times your eyes are hollow looking if not, empty. David that causes me to lose sleep at night. You have a power far beyond anyone I have ever known. You sir, are truly gifted!

    Me: Well thanks buddy boy, but one of the gifts I don't possess is the gift of time. So now we're going to move on to, "Brothers of The Tattered Cloth." My goal in writing that book was to point out the sameness within all of our differences, how's that for a twist? We all have a past and as in most people's pasts (whether you want to admit it or not) we all have had a bit of darkness. It's not at all about where we come from, it's where we're going. So with the two

Catholic Priests, they have both been proven to be what, liars, cheaters and profound manipulators? I want to see the first one here to go ahead and raise your hand as to any of you being the exception. Who's not ever lied, not ever cheated or not ever manipulated? Go ahead but if I see a hand in the air you're going to be dismissed. That's right, we are all human beings, just like those two Priests who had the greatest of intentions but it took them a great amount of time struggling to get to that point of their great intentions.

So, it's about winning the battle, it's about developing the courage necessary to win that battle. The battle that lives deep within ourselves!

Kids we're not going to review my sixth book, "#belikead." The reason being is that I had a co-author who I promoted as a fledgling author, who has now become an author all on her own and she's doing quite well. I couldn't tell you how proud I am of her but that book doesn't belong in this mix. So kids let's get to the book that brought us all here to this dance, "The Judicial System is Guilty the Raping of Lady Justice."

First of all, I want to see the hands in the air that didn't like this book. Go ahead put your hands up high in the air if you didn't like this book then gather your shit and I will have security escort you off the floor and out of this fucking building. If you've noticed, I have not asked any of you of your political party affiliations. I don't care about that and if I didn't need you all, I wouldn't be meeting with you. Yes, I'm well aware that I went after some heavy power brokers by name and now six months after that book has been published many of the things that I spoke of have come to fruition and made national headlines. Many of the things that I made assertions to, will now be supported in a court of law. Oh yeah a whole bunch of thieving fuckers are going down and those people are scared shitless. That's the whole reason why we're here isn't it kids? This book is what started this fire and this fire has now become the blazing inferno of the century. They're going to try to soft pedal it and that's why we're all sitting here so they can hang me and go about their merry ways with even more corruption.

    Damn it Fredy, how many times in the last three minutes have you shuffled your feet or crossed and uncrossed your arms? Jesus Christ settle down son, what is it that's got your panties in a bundle?

    Frederic: David, I'm so glad we finally got to this, for my money I think the most important of all accusations that they can possibly make against you is whether or not you murdered your friend, Heck Ramsey.

    Me: Freddy you prick, you went after the easy meat! So you're going to spend the rest of your law career and life, gathering the low-hanging fruit and become nothing more than an ambulance chaser? Jesus Christ man grow some balls, would you please? Yeah word has it that you're somewhat of a fighter or is that just your front to appear like you're some kind of power broker? Well chum, at this point you're not the sun or the moon. You're not much of anything beyond your pompous attitude. Hopefully you will fill out the front of your underwear and grow some actual balls.

    Let's move on. How about all the other assertions I made about racism by thieving the Black Lives Matter leaders, how about the assertions I made about social workers being manipulative thieves, how about the assertion of the politicians who knew damn well what was going on with the Minnesota's, 'Feed the Children' program and turned a blind eye because why? Because it's a power base that they will need to have to keep the Democratic party in control. But we fooled them a bit with that blind eye stuff. My few Pals and I, brought it to the feds, it is damn hard to trust our federal government these days and who the fuck does? I don't know where any of it's going to go but at least it's been exposed and a number of arrests have been made. What I would like to see investigated is what the hell happened to 'Woodland Hills', the children's behavioral inpatient long term, treatment center here in Duluth. After a 118-year run, they suddenly locked their doors and dumped one hundred and sixteen or more children who were all cast to the four winds! Tell me that's not a, what the fuck moment! There most definitely was some dirt there but nothing's come out, nothing may ever come out of it because thieves protect thieves for fear of themselves being exposed. If there's ever truly an investigation, many of Duluth's,

"Do Gooders" and socialites will be making little rocks from big rocks.

Fred, I will get back to you in a few minutes, I'll give you some time to center yourself.

Wyatt you're the man, you want to be the Top Cop and you want to run the show, so I'm going to toss you this hot potato. Try not to drop it, how you slice it and dice it and serve it up, will have everything to do with your entire future. So now it's game on, my friend, what's your take on page fifty of "The Judicial System is Guilty" you know page fifty which follows all the way through to page 108 and runs through a couple of different chapters. Five chapters and fifty-eight pages to be exact. What do you think? Was Heck Ramsey's heartache so terribly real that I was so deeply impacted by it, that I was the one that gave him the ink pen and told him what to do with it? I did tell him to go back to his cell and write his story. Was my emptying out the three attorney's briefcases and destroying all of their writing instruments a ploy to shift everyone's suspicions away from me to hide my guilt? Was that all part of my master plan? Did I lead my readers into believing that one of those three attorneys were responsible? Wyatt, what is your take on it? Give me what you got buddy and don't hold anything back. This my friend is when you slip into your big boy pants. I want you to play, "The Devil's Advocate." I want you to speak in the voice of the opposition. I want you to be the chief prosecutor, I want you to come at me and I'll do my best to remember that we're all just role playing and I'll do my very, very best to keep my gun in its holster and refrain from shooting you. It's time for you to get nasty ole son. You got the stage pal, bring it!

Wyatt: Jesus Christ David, you got my guts so knotted up that I hope I never have to go up against a guy like you in court. I know exactly what I want to say, how and where I want to say it, but could you give me a few minutes just to compose myself?

Me: Sure, buddy take all your time you need, for the next five minutes but remember that this isn't fucking Romper Room. This is real life shit with real life big people, if you don't get your game on now, you'll never have a game. This is your proving ground my friend, it's time to shine. You have five minutes to prep, you can go sit in my office but don't touch any of my shit and yes, there's alarms and cameras everywhere. If you still feel weepy after that I will send you out to one of those massage parlors that offer a happy ending. I understand that they take credit cards these days so you should be in good shape, now get out of my sight!

Amy: Hell David, I guess I've been worrying about the wrong person having a heart attack, what you just did with poor Wyatt is insane, you just showed him that he's not what he thought he was, you all but crushed him! You were kind enough to give him a chance to catch his breath but I suggest you might want to go easy on him, remember that you guys are all in this together, he is an ally.

Me: Is he an ally or is he a plant, is he batting for the other team? We're about to find out, aren't we my dear?

Amy: So, David this is how you're going to vet him? Yeah, what's a better test than trial by fire, do you have a flame thrower hidden in your kitchen junk drawer, the same place where you keep, "The Noise?"

Me: He's just God damn lucky I don't make him walk barefoot across a blazing hot bed of coals! So let me tell you this youngster, I love you sweetheart but don't get in the middle of my business. *Capiche?*

Amy sat back in her chair and lowered her head. All I could think of was, "Son of a bitch, I just broke another one." Here's another one I have to cuddle or coddle. What happened to this toughness thing that's supposed to be part of the human experience? All I see around here is a bunch of weaklings who've been protected and coddled all of their lives, it seems as though no one has ever had to fight for anything, they all are about to learn how to fight. I needed another walk so I went to find a walking partner.

Chapter 21
First Gear

Wyatt: David, I don't even know where to begin. How can I play The Devil's Advocate when I would lay my life down for you?

Me: Son you're a lawyer, the word lawyer and liar are quite close together both in sound and oftentimes in definition, perhaps the word synonymous would be more fitting? Do your best young man, who knows, someday you may want to be a real prosecutor. If you get into a very large dispute and you want to crush somebody regardless of the effect it may have on them, just think back on this day and my smiling face. Okay enough patty cake what have you got?

Wyatt: No offense to anyone but I would like to have a few moments to speak with David in private. David can we go for one of your patented walks?

Me: I'm not quite sure that you don't have snipers up on the roof or maybe a car will come careening up on the sidewalk and take me out like a bowling pin. What is it you have to say that can't be heard by your fellow solicitors? So, the hard answer is no. Wyatt, you got shit to put on the table, put it on the table so we can all examine it.

Suddenly I heard the entry door open to my Suite and in walked Minnesota State Supreme Court Justice Thompson along with my pal Tim!
Well, here's another what the fuck moment! The judge smiled as Tim said, "David, your phone is going to ring in 30 seconds, you will want to answer it."

The call back number came up as Amanda's cell phone.

Amanda: Good afternoon sweetheart, I hope my call finds you well? I will get right to the point. I want to congratulate you for standing your ground in this entire matter. These people were under the impression that you were the low-hanging fruit, well you most certainly did give them a run for their money. I love the way you dragged them through your not so "Enchanted Forest", kudos to you!
These people that you're currently sitting with other than Amy and Wyatt are not who you may think they are. Yes, they are all attorneys but they work for an organization that is not well known. The FBI has a separate and secret body that investigates political corruption and money laundering. Your information will be held in the strictest of confidence. I'm sorry my

dear but if you knew that they were FBI investigators from the beginning, you would have told them all to all go bite a fart (your words) and walked away.

I myself was not surprised as to how quickly you got on to them, you just didn't quite know what the 'on to them' meant. At the time you were right to suspect and carry the assumptions that there may be moles in your group and you were wicked quick to wonder if they may not even be a seated investigative panel that wanted to put you away.

What you have done is you have just supplied your testimony to the U.S. Department of Justice as a protected informant. There will be no further need for any more meetings with any of these people. You can either shake their hands, give them hugs, take them to dinner or throw them out but please don't throw them out any windows. Now I would officially like to turn your life back over to you. I can now be your friend again. I'll be out next week, hopefully Heather and you will have cooled off by then. But for now goodbye sweetheart, I'll talk to you next week.

The phone line went dead. The lawyers / Undercover FBI agents all stood. Doris had the biggest smile of them all and she said, "I'm hoping you will shake my hand and even give me a hug but if you choose not to, I and we will all understand."

Me: So, you want a hug from me, sweetheart? You better know that I'm going to grab your butt, come on baby let's have a hug.

It was handshakes, hugs and laughter all around. I called down to Bar Service and ordered the very same bottles of wine that those people tried to smuggle into my loft that I gave away a week or so ago. Yep, we had a party that night.

Chapter 22
The Threesome

I slept poorly that night and I knew exactly what it was. I had some unfinished business with Amy and Phillis that I needed to clean up with before I could send them off on their way. I called them at 4am and told them to brush their hair and their teeth, put on some comfy clothes and call me as you're standing at the elevator. In the next 10 minutes and I'll come down and get you two. Of course, they were both a bit hungover from the night before and that's just the way I wanted it. It couldn't be a more perfect setting.

Me: Girls there's fresh coffee in this carafe. Have a donut, sit back and listen while you drink your coffee. There's something nagging at me, there's something more between you two and I'd like to know what it is. Who wants to start?

They both looked at each other not knowing what the hell I was talking about. I could see them almost thinking of what more could be left. I smiled inwardly.

    Me: Girls there is something more, tell me about where your lives are going to take you now. Phyllis you still want to be a practicing attorney, locked into law books and courtrooms sending out dozens upon dozens of emails, reading blue backs and all the other bullshit that comes along with it or do you want to live your life? Nothing different for you either Amy girl. Is this the life you want, sitting listening to other people's troubles all fucking day long, writing volume after volume of weepy bullshit clinical notes, on people who just aren't willing to deal with themselves or do you have future plans? Well kids, I've got a plan for the both of you. You are all but joined at the hip, the two of you need to go on sabbatical. I don't know where the hell a sabbatical is even located but you need to go there and what will you do when you're on or at sabbatical, is that you're going to write a book. Not to honor me but a book of what you have learned from the first day that you recall in life to this very moment. You do know there's other people like you too that are so locked into their careers, their professions or whatever the fuck they're locked into but nobody knows how to breathe. I want to send you on a journey where you learn how to breathe, after all what's the worst that could happen? You gals certainly already do have well-developed lungs in that frontal region I might say. But you don't know how to breathe. Talk to me girls.

Amy: David, I'll tell on the both of us. We listen to a lot of the music that you have suggested of your era. The music that was comforting and healing for you. We found so many different lyrics that speak of you. One of our all-time favorites (although there are many) but our favorite is from Rod Stewart and his song, "I don't want to talk about it." David I would like to come over and kneel before you and no, this is not a sexual thing and I'm not here to show my adornment of you. I just want to hold my hand on your heart. Lean back in your chair and please spread your legs.

Of course, I wanted to ask what the fuck this shit's all about. Now you've taken over and you're going to tell me how things are going to go? Did they forget who invited them or in all honesty who ordered them to be here at this moment, did they forget that shit?

Phil: David we have listened to that song dozens and dozens and dozens of times both alone and together and it speaks so much of you. Even the first line. "I can tell by your eyes that you've probably been crying forever." That fully describes you but you've cried in silence and without tears for most all of your life. I have to guess that's where some if not all of your life's failures come from.

Amy: We have tried to plan a time for us three to get together and have this very conversation but we didn't want to upset you and we felt that you were probably done with us after our going-away party last night and I do have to say, that wine was the best that

I've ever drank. So you just told us that you want us to learn how to breathe. David, we would like to tell you that we would like to teach you how to cry. There's great healing power in letting your tears flow. It brings you to a neutral place to where you can feel what's in your heart and then heal yourself. Does that make sense to you babe?

    Me: Of course, that makes sense and I do that with Heather, I've done it a few times with some of the people that I sponsor through AA or some AA members with a hurting heart. Yes, we embrace, we share a few quiet tears and we tell each other that we love each other. It's not just tears that give us a release, it's the way we look at each other. Sober alcoholics can say volumes with just a look. So, kids, I appreciate our chat very much but we're not going to sit here holding hands and have a cry fest. What we're going to do is go downstairs and have some breakfast but not until you go back to your rooms and pretty yourself up for your flights home. I do want one more glimpse of the hotties that I'll never see the likes of ever again in my lifetime. Come on kids, I'll take you back to your rooms. Short dresses and hooker heels are the order of this day!

Chapter 23
Avery's Coming Out Party

    I sat with Avery for several days outlining her new book. She's even brighter than I thought she was. We talked about how sad she was when her father became sick and eventually passed. How at first, she felt somehow responsible like she should have been enough to keep him going. She felt like she let him down and at some point, the worm turned and she said she was angry with her daddy for leaving her all alone in this world. She talked about her loneliness and her sorrow and why she became a ghost and it was a simple matter of, "My daddy didn't want me so I guess nobody else does either."

    I knew it was time that I told my truths, for me and Avery, maybe for all of mankind.

    Me: Avery my dear heart, I've tried to bring you to this point to give you relief and to release the ghost in your life and to never allow it to return. I'm sure you wonder how I've gathered all this knowledge or wisdom or whatever else you want to call it. You see babe, I too have had a ghost in my locker for many, many years. In part, you and I hosted the very same ghost. The sameness of our ghosts is that you hid your loneliness and sorrow by withdrawing from people. Whereas I hid those very same feelings by being a bully to keep people away from me. My ghost was different, much different than your ghost. You carried shame and sorrow; I carried hate and rage. My ghost was destroying me, your ghost was holding you back. We both had to take a level of action far beyond our grasp but yet we knew it was our only hope.

Understand this, where we come from and what happened in our young life's sweetheart is not our fault, where we go with it, is our responsibility and if we fail, it's our fault. We have a choice to leave it lie and let it eat us from the inside like a wood tick or re-examine our efforts and take action and move forward my darling child. Speaking of moving forward my dear, you're not going to veterinary school to become a veterinarian's assistant. If you're an assistant all you get to do is whatever the vet tells you to do. It's like being a nurse, you don't get to make any real decisions, you just do what you're told and only what you're told. You have a deeper heart than that, you have to decide on the animals' healthcare and how you can best serve your patient. No baby, you're not going to become a vet-tech you are going to become a veterinarian, as in DVM! All of your educational and living expenses are taken care of through a foundation that well knows of young people's struggles and the importance of realizing their dreams.

We made some great headway in those few days. I was quite proud of her efforts.

Amanda did come into town and spent two nights at our house. I wanted very much for her to come to the assembly and meet Avery. Of course, that was met with a warm smile as she said, "This is you buddy, all of this is on you. Yes, we'll take care of her tuition and her and her mother's living expenses in Colorado. That was a very nice touch with offering them a new life. I guess it's pretty easy to be kind when you're spending other people's money, you prick!"

The morning of Denfeld High School's all class assembly was a chili and windy day but it did nothing to dampen my spirits. I don't ever remember feeling this good about myself and the world around me. Heather and I arrived at the school one hour early. I met with the school principal for a brief chat and I struck out to find Avery. The principal escorted us into Avery's class. Avery bolted from her chair and threw her arms around my neck and kissed both of my cheeks as she whispered, "I still can't believe this is happening!" I just smiled, reached out my hand and said come with me, we're going for a bit of a stroll. We walked around the outside of the school proper as I told her about a bit of a change in the schedule.

Me: Sweetheart, here's what's actually going to happen today. Your principal, along with the superintendent of schools and our mayor will all be on the stage with us. Your principal will introduce me and I in turn will introduce you. I'm not going to speak much about my writing, I'm going to speak about your writing and you my lady is going to speak about your new book, "The Ghost Who Steps from My Locker."

Now I probably shouldn't be telling you this but the superintendent of schools has his own announcement to make. I'm telling you this now so you don't freak out at the time but here's what's going to happen. The superintendent is going to announce that your book will become mandatory reading in every class in the entire School District! That's 26 schools and over 8,358 students. You, my sweet child after today, will become the ghost of the past!

It took nearly 10 minutes for all the dignitary introductions and all of the important things these people thought they had to say, as though it was their time and not Avery's. In the grand scheme of all things political, there stood a handful of adults riding on a 17-year-old girls shirt tails. I did a brief description of my experience within the Duluth School District as a student and how a failing student grew to become a broken man and how that broken man through the help of many others learned to heal himself and then brought his blessings forward to help others heal with his writings.

When I finished, I got to introduce Avery to her fellow students. I talked a bit about how we met and where Avery is today. When I repeated the announcement of Avery's book was going to be required reading for the entire student body of the entire School District there were gasps throughout the audience. Obviously, no one knew of, "The ghost in her locker."

For a 17-year-old kid, Avery carried herself well and spoke quite eloquently of her writing project. She spoke for almost 20 minutes, no stammering, no hesitation. Here before the whole world, a young lady stood, who knew exactly who she is and where she is going. The Applause from the entire student body was deafening. I was a very proud man with tears in my eyes.

Students and staff rushed the stage to congratulate Avery and I was almost swept off the stage which was fine with me. This was Avery's moment, the moment that she grew her wings!

I had one more thing to take care of before I became a truly free man. I called Tim while I was waiting to get through the crowd of the auditorium. Tim answered with a giggle. There was a lot of background noise of different levels of people's voices.

Me: Where the hell are you?

Tim: Watching you getting your shoes scuffed in this crowd. I'm at the main auditorium exit doors. Tell those people all around you that you're a bigshot and they need to make way! I'm waiting for you.

If there is one common denominator amongst all Minnesota people is that no one knows how to say goodbye. People here just can't say, "so long or see you later" nope! They all have to stand in everyone's way to tell you what their entire family is doing, how their last doctor visit went, kids and grandkids sports followed by them firing up their cellphone to show you and the world of the fish they caught, the grouse and deer killed last season and their pets wearing those ridiculous pointed paper party hats right down to the fucking rubber band under their pets chin!

Tim: I almost pulled the fire alarm to get these people moving!
Me: I'm damn glad that you didn't. While I was trying to slip through this mosh pit, I found out that little Mary just had her first period. Billy made the football team's second string. Someone's neighbor is a drunk that is screwing the neighbor's wife from across the street and Kenny lost his job for coming to work too drunk to do his job. I feel so fucking enriched! Walk with me.

We walked to the football field and I led him to the bleachers. I took him to the top and we sat next to the press box and announcer's booth.

Me: I have been thinking about a way to say goodbye to you. I was not at all surprised to find that you were in the auditorium today. You told me several months ago that you wanted to hang out with me to learn how to knock off some of your rough edges so you could be a better daddy. Well Dink, I have found that you've been playing me. As you probably already know, I've been spending some time with Avery. She unknowingly told on you. I understand that you have taken Avery to the "Daddy / Daughter Dance" for the last four years. Don't even try to slip away from that, she proudly showed me a hefty stack of pictures. You take her to the circus every year, you take her fishing on Minnesota's fishing season opener, you guys go to ball games, go-karting and eat hot dogs once every month. Explain yourself.

Tim: Four years ago I was walking by Alana's office and I heard her crying. I stepped in and asked her what the problem was. She told me about her daughter missing her deceased daddy especially with the upcoming, "Daddy / Daughter Dance." The rest is history. Getting to know you in the last three years and reading your book, "Daddy had to Say Goodbye" and the loss of your baby and your dreams, told me I needed to up my game with my girls. In short Skippy, you don't get to say goodbye to me. I will be with you until the end. What do you say we find Heather and grab some lunch?

Me: Not so fast sport. Tell me, what did you think with all of the students that went up onto the stage to be with Avery, what did you see?

Tim: With the way you're asking that, I guess I must have missed something. Okay old wise one, what did I miss?

Me: What you missed my friend, was that those kids didn't rush the stage just to be with Avery. They went on that stage knowing that they also have ghosts in their lockers which they can't admit to. Another part of those kids were there to dump their own shame for mistreating and bullying her.

Obviously, I've given you far too much credit for being a learnerd student, yeah maybe you better stick around for a while.

The three of us went for lunch. On the way home (Heather drove) I reached into my pocket and took my truck keys into my hand. Just as we were pulling into the garage Heather said. "I know where you're going sweetheart, say hello to Saundra for me."

I stopped at a flower shop and drove on to the cemetery to visit with my baby girl.

THE END

To contact the author, David J Brown please email: David J. Brown@gmail.com

To order David's first audiobook and his other eight novels please visit David's website at: davidjbrownbooks.com

Book #1: "Daddy Had to Say Goodbye: A Story of Hope."

Book #2: "Flesh of a Fraud: The Lies We Tell Ourselves"

Book #3: "Altered Egos: The killers In Us All"

Book #4: "Harvest Season: Body Parts"

Book #5: "Brothers of The Tattered Cloth"

Book #6: "The Judicial System is Guilty the Raping of Lady Justice"

Book #7: "Betrayed: My Body Is Killing Me"

Book #8: "The Ghost In Our Lockers"

Book #9: "#Be Like Ed"

Made in the USA
Monee, IL
01 March 2024